WHEN THE TIDES CHANGE

BY
HANNAH WERNER

Chapter 1

"I wish his wife would disappear," Lexy Price snickered at the idea of it. Her platinum blonde hair tossed in the wind as she strolled along The Battery in downtown Charleston with her best friend, Nora Bellinger. Historical mansions were on display to the right of them, and the Charleston Harbor was to the left. Either direction they looked, the view was spectacular.

Nora's eyes narrowed and a small, vertical wrinkle appeared between her eyebrows. The striking brunette was clearly annoyed by the boldness of her best friend. "Don't say that," Nora ordered. "You could have anyone you want, why do you want a married man?" Her question was answered by Lexy's rolling eyes.

The smoky orange color of the sky reminded them that the sun was going to set soon. There was nothing like the relief of the sun disappearing below the horizon on a hot, summer day in Charleston, South Carolina. Lexy's skimpy yellow dress hiked up her tan leg as she walked, drawing the attention of anyone who crossed her path.

A man walking by with his family did a dramatic double-take when he saw the two women. He let his eyes linger on the young ladies for far too long. His wife blushed next to him; she was painfully aware of his wandering eyes. Lexy and Nora couldn't help but giggle. They knew the effect they had on men, and they enjoyed the attention they received.

While they wandered into White Point Gardens, Lexy told Nora about her upcoming plans. "George is taking me to Los Angeles with him. He has a medical conference there for the week, and he wants me to come along with him," Lexy bragged. George was a doctor at the Medical University of South Carolina which is where Lexy met him while employed as a nurse. Once they found themselves involved in their secret relationship, George convinced her to find a new job away from the medical university. He insisted that the risk of them getting caught was too high if they continued to work together. Determined to continue their relationship, Lexy agreed and found a new job as a nurse at a primary care practice in Mount Pleasant. "I can't wait until we can act like a real couple. Even if it's only for a few days, it will be nice to be able to hold hands without the fear of running into his psycho wife or one of her nosy friends."

Nora crossed her arms in front of her chest, "You don't know she's a psychopath. She could very well be a cool lady. How do you know he isn't madly in love with her and using you for the hell of it?" Lexy ignored Nora's question. Of course, Lexy had already considered that possibility. George claimed he didn't love Penelope, but Lexy knew that most men tell women exactly what they want to hear. It was possible that he still loved his wife. It didn't make a difference to Lexy either way. He was spending his free time with Lexy, and that's all that mattered to her.

During the beginning of their affair, Lexy had stalked Penelope's Facebook profile. She wanted to see what Penelope looked like, and more importantly, she wanted to see pictures of George and Penelope Thompson together. Penelope was stunning; she was truly a classic beauty. They were a handsome power couple. Though, according to George, Penelope was controlling and cold. George loved Lexy's carefree, wild nature. He had no plans to leave his wife, and Lexy knew that. They had never had a formal conversation about it, but she knew he wasn't going to give up his posh existence. He and his wife had the perfect Lowcountry life. He wasn't going to abandon that for Lexy. As confident as she was, she wasn't stupid.

"I've been saving up my PTO at work, and I could use a vacation. Don't burst my bubble, Nora." The two best friends had a handful of similar conversations in the past. Lexy had a habit of picking the wrong guys, especially married guys, and it never ended well. She was always left heart-broken, and Nora was always left picking up the pieces. "He makes me happy, and that's all I care about right now. I know it's not going to lead anywhere."

Nora grabbed Lexy's hand and interlocked their fingers, "You know I want you to be happy. I support you, but it's also my job to be straight forward with you. And honestly, I think we need a drink." Nora waved to a man nearby on a rickshaw, a common bike taxi in downtown Charleston.

"And some food," Lexy added to Nora's suggestion.

The man operating the rickshaw appeared in front of them within seconds, overly enthusiastic to offer his services to the two beautiful women. Nora playfully flirted with him as she climbed into the taxi, and Lexy followed suit. He chatted with the two women while he biked, and he effortlessly took them to their requested location, The Rarebit. They were both impressed by his physical abilities; he was barely winded from the almost two-mile bike ride. He slipped Nora his phone number, and he insisted there was no charge for the ride.

"Are you going to call him?" Lexy asked Nora as the hostess led them to an open booth inside their destination. They both enjoyed the eclectic vibe The Rarebit offered; it was one of their go-to spots seeing as it was only a couple of blocks from Lexy's apartment.

"I might, he was cute. I could use that athleticism in the bedroom." Nora winked at Lexy before directing her attention to the cocktail menu. Nora was into fun, younger guys while Lexy was constantly searching for deeper, more mature men. Though, in reality, Nora typically ended up with guys who were jobless and living at home with their parents, and Lexy almost always ended up with married men. They were never wildly impressed with the options they found, and neither of the women had ever been in long-term relationships. To put it nicely, they had terrible taste in men.

The waitress brought their drinks over only a few minutes after they ordered them. "Cheers!" The best friends said in unison, toasting to each other. They spent the rest of the evening huddled in the booth together, watching the other patrons while they downed snacks and cocktails. A variety of men made their way to their booth throughout the night, but none of them were invited to sit down with them. The women were unimpressed over and over again, and they would quickly shoo the men away. At the end of the night, they walked back to Lexy's apartment together, pleased with their uneventful girls' night.

The two best friends would typically end up

back at Lexy's apartment after a night out. Nora rented a cute condo on Isle of Palms, and although it was fun for beach days, it was a trek after a night of drinking downtown. Nora had a drawer in Lexy's bathroom, which stored a toothbrush, face wash, and other toiletries. She spent the night there at least once a week. Lexy had the same set-up at Nora's, for the long beach days and island party nights. The title of best friends was an understatement; Nora and Lexy were more like sisters.

Not ready to end their night, the two stayed up watching episodes of Real Housewives. Eventually, they both made their way to Lexy's king-sized bed. The following morning, Lexy woke to find Nora already out of bed, and the smell of pancakes was in the air. After wrapping herself in a pink satin robe, she made her way to the kitchen she rarely put to use.

"Mmm! Those smell amazing," Lexy squealed as she greeted her best friend. "Why can't you be a man?" She headed to the refrigerator to pour herself a glass of orange juice.

Nora smirked, "You know, you could easily make pancakes. It's not hard. You have a nice kitchen, and I'm pretty sure I'm the only one who uses the stovetop. You should do some exploring in here."

"Oh trust me, I've explored the kitchen," Lexy

motioned with her hips, making Nora throw her head back in laughter. Making her way to the kitchen table with her orange juice in hand, Lexy slid into a chair. She sat with her knees to her chest, patiently waiting for her breakfast. Their friendship dynamic might have been strange to some, but it worked for them.

Nora brought a plate stacked with soft, fluffy pancakes over to the table, "Dig in!" Lexy did as she was told. After enjoying her pancakes drowned in maple syrup, Lexy's stomach couldn't handle another bite. She cleared the table and began doing the dishes.

"I hate leaving you with the rest of the dishes, but I need to head out," Nora said as she gathered her things. "I have some errands to run, laundry to do, and a meeting bright and early tomorrow morning. Will you text me when you land in Los Angeles? I know you'll be busy but please try to remember. Please. I'll be worried about you." Lexy hugged her best friend and promised to keep in touch with her before Nora headed out the door. While she finished the dishes in silence, Lexy imagined how her upcoming trip with George would be. She couldn't wait to have alone time with him; they hadn't seen each other in over a week.

With a laundry basket full of dirty clothes and an empty suitcase that desperately needed to be packed, Lexy put a Spotify playlist on shuffle and cranked up the speakers in her bedroom. She packed far more than she needed; she wanted to be ready for whatever George had planned for their trip. In less than twenty-four hours, she would be on vacation with the married man she was in love with.

Chapter 2

George and Penelope Thompson had been together for over fifteen years. Blissfully married for almost ten years, their relationship appeared to be solid. George had his career as a doctor at MUSC, and Penelope owned a small, successful boutique in downtown Charleston. To anyone on the outside looking in, they were a happy couple. Some might even say they were a perfect couple, but those people didn't know the dark secrets George harbored. George had been unfaithful for a couple of years. He made sure to be discreet with his affairs, and Penelope was seemingly unaware of his deceit.

Penelope always packed George's suitcase for his out of town trips. "Your suitcase is by the bedroom door and ready to go," she informed him while she reached over to adjust his tie. Penelope was a perfectionist, and their home reflected that. The Thompson's lived in a beautiful house in the Old Village in Mount Pleasant. They had a view of the Arthur Ravenel Jr. Bridge from their backyard pool, and a beautiful dock that led into the

Charleston Harbor. The Thompson's loved host-
ing parties, and their house was a frequent gather-
ing spot for their friends.

"You're too good to me, Penelope," George
proclaimed, all while knowing it was perfectly
true. Penelope was a doting wife, and he was a
cheating pig. Occasionally, George would reconsider his actions, sometimes even regret them. He
loved Penelope, and he didn't want to hurt her.
Once he had started the affairs, he found it difficult to stop. Women flocked to him; his career and
marital status seemed to easily influence younger
women. He liked how they looked at him. Penelope saw herself as an equal to George, whereas his
floozies saw him as a god. The attention was something he couldn't give up. He was addicted to it.

George kissed his wife goodbye before he
climbed into his Mercedes S-Class Coupe. Penelope mouthed "I love you" to him right before he
drove away, a silent message that stung his heart.
He had a good woman; a woman who loved him.
Why did he do this to her? He contemplated the
reasoning behind his infidelities while driving to
pick up his mistress. No matter how hard he tried,
he couldn't blame it on Penelope. She was the
kind of wife any man would dream of having; she
was magical. He loved her, and he knew he would
never leave her.

In the past, most of his flings didn't inquire

about his marriage, but Lexy was curious from the start. George lied to Lexy; he told her that Penelope was miserable to be around. That couldn't have been further from the truth. The truth was: George was selfish. George wanted his picture-perfect wife with a side of whatever flavor of the week that happened to catch his interest.

Shortly after George parallel parked on Lexy's street, she ran out to embrace him. He shushed her while he gracefully removed her arms from his body. They snuck inside her apartment before he carefully checked the street for anyone who might have seen them. "You need to be more careful, Lexy! I have colleagues downtown!"

Lexy ignored him, shoving her suitcase towards him, "Let's go, baby. We have a flight to catch!" She kissed him on the cheek before she ushered him out. After locking her apartment door, she slipped into the passenger seat of his car. She had only been in it a handful of times and was always amazed by the grandeur of the interior.

George joined Lexy in the car and slid one of his large hands onto her bare thigh. "Everything is loaded. Are you ready?" Lexy nodded, offering him a smile. She looked almost hesitant, but he knew how she felt about him. He had her wrapped around his finger.

The drive from Lexy's apartment to the airport was about fifteen minutes, but on that day, it took them over an hour. An accident on the small stretch of interstate they needed to take to get to the airport caused the unwanted delay. "We still have two hours until our flight. We'll be fine," Lexy reassured George while she checked the traffic on her phone. They had never spent more than one consecutive evening together; an entire trip was something out of the ordinary for them.

Once they arrived at the airport, everything started to look up for Lexy. She assumed they would be flying coach. To her surprise, George had purchased first-class tickets. Cozy in their first-class seats, they sipped wine and whispered. Over time, they got a little too touchy-feely for their seat neighbors, resulting in some unwanted stares. It didn't stop them. They took their fun to the bathroom and joined the mile-high club. Laughing off the judgmental looks on the walk of shame back to their seats, they ordered more wine before drifting off into booze-induced naps.

"Please take your seats and prepare for landing," a flight attendant with an extremely high-pitched voice announced, waking up both Lexy and George.

"The conference had arranged for a driver to pick me up from the airport. I wanted to be more discreet than that though, so I got a rental car. We will be staying at a hotel separate from the conference so you can enjoy yourself any way you see fit." George told Lexy as they prepared to disembark. "After we check-in at the hotel, I have to head to a few meetings."

Lexy, visibly disappointed, reasoned with George, "I thought we were spending time together on this trip." He ignored her efforts to pout as they got off the plane and retrieved their luggage. Although he found her pouting childish and pathetic, he knew she would give over it soon enough. Once in the rental car, Lexy sent a quick text to Nora to let her know she had made it to California. Nora was relieved to hear from her and wished her a wonderful trip.

George drove in silence, and Lexy felt as if the trip was already off to a bad start. The tension between them was unbearable, and Lexy knew she had to clear the air. She finally spoke up, "I understand you are here for a conference. I can wait. Just know, I'll be lonely, probably naked, and bored with you gone." She was partially joking, but she was curious to see how he would respond. She had always used her sexuality for manipulation. Nine times out of ten, it had worked.

"I'll be rushing back to the room after my meeting," George promised. He knew he would get what he wanted when he wanted it; he could wait which meant Lexy would have to as well. His conference was the reason why they had traveled to Los Angeles; the least he could do was go to the

13

meetings he was scheduled to attend. "We're almost to the hotel. We'll check-in to our room and get you settled before I head out."

Entering the Millenium Biltmore Hotel, Lexy was mesmerized. "You didn't tell me we were staying in a castle!" She screamed like a five-year-old girl seeing Disney World for the first time. The hotel's interior was a beautiful mixture of European styles, including Renaissance and Neo-classical. The architecture was magnificent; Lexy could hardly believe she would be sleeping there.

"It's not a castle; it's a hotel. Tone it down a bit," George spoke to her as if she were a child. "You need to appear to fit in with these people." Lexy didn't let George know it, but his words hurt her. She knew she wasn't as classy or well-to-do as him or his wife, but at that moment, she realized how George saw her. To him, she was a cheap mistress. She was Julia Roberts in Pretty Woman, you know, without the hooker part. She didn't fit into his world, and she never would.

While George checked them in, the concierge informed Lexy that the Millennium Biltmore Hotel's ballroom, the Biltmore Bowl, was the site of eight Oscar ceremonies during the 1930s and 1940s. Lexy was still awestruck when George joined her at the concierge desk. "Can I offer any recommendations, Sir? What about a nice restaurant to take this lovely lady?" The concierge politely suggested.

"We have tonight sorted out," George groped Lexy, making it clear to the concierge that they would be busy for the evening.

"Thank you for all the cool information, Jake!" Lexy said politely.

The attractive concierge smiled back at her. "I'll be here if you need me," he said before winking at her. George saw his gesture and guided Lexy towards the elevators.

"Was that frat boy hitting on you?" he asked. George had never shown any jealousy before. For some reason, Lexy felt flattered.

She entered the empty elevator and pressed the button for the fifth floor before responding to George's absurd question. "Why would it matter?" she asked. "You're married, remember."

In response, George grabbed her and pushed her up against the elevator wall. "While you're here with me, you're mine. Got that?" He whispered in her ear before aggressively kissing her lips. She met his kiss with a fiery passion. Moments later, the elevator door opened to two wide-eyed strangers. Grabbing their suitcases, George and Lexy ran out of the elevator, tittering like teenagers.

Once they were alone in their extravagant hotel room, their clothes went flying off their bodies. Within no time, their room was filled with sounds of pleasure. "I knew you would stick around for a little while," Lexy bragged, rolling over onto her side.

"That was amazing," George admitted while putting his pants back on. "I want to spend time with you. That is why I brought you here with me," he explained. "I have to attend my meetings though. It's part of the deal. I promise I won't be gone long. Try to enjoy yourself! Order whatever you want for dinner." He kissed her lightly on the lips before heading out the door. Maybe Lexy wasn't as classy as Penelope, but she was the one there with George. That had to mean something.

With George gone, Lexy quickly noticed her hunger. She took the liberty of ordering a pizza from a nearby pizzeria. Jake, the concierge, brought the pizza up to her room when it was delivered to the front desk. He initially intended to flirt with her, but she didn't give him the chance. She respected that she was there with George.

With a belly full of pizza and a newly released movie playing on the television, Lexy dozed off. "Wake up," a deep voice whispered in her ear hours after she drifted off to sleep. She groaned, turning over to greet the man standing over her.

"George, climb into bed with me." The married man slipped under the scratchy hotel sheets with his naked mistress.

Chapter 3

The next morning, Lexy woke to George rounding the corner with a tray loaded full of bagels, muffins, and other pastries. He must have snuck down to the Rendezvous Court, the hotel café. He plopped the tray of pastries down onto the bed, and Lexy's stomach growled. She had never had that kind of treatment. George spoiled her. He made her feel wanted, and that's the feeling Lexy was endlessly searching for.

They ate their breakfast in bed and watched the news. "Do you have any meetings to attend this morning?" Lexy finally asked, not really wanting to hear George's answer.

George got up and started heading towards the bathroom. "I do have a few," he admitted. "I need to shower and head out." He turned on the water, testing the temperature. "I'll be done with my meetings for the day by one o'clock. We can spend the afternoon together doing whatever you want." Lexy's face lit up. Moments after George entered the walk-in shower, she joined him. She wanted to make sure that he would be thinking of her while he was gone.

As George put on his suit and tie, Lexy sprawled out on the bed. "Don't get your wet hair on the pillow," George commanded, making Lexy reposition herself. "I scheduled a massage for you at the hotel spa. It's at ten. I thought you could use some relaxation. I'll see you back here at one." She barely got a chance to thank him before he left their room.

Lexy had never had a professional massage before. She was excited, but she also felt slightly uncomfortable going into it. She didn't know what to expect. The moment she met her masseuse, all of her worries drifted away. "Mrs. Thompson, you're next!" A woman shouted. Lexy looked around the room before realizing the petite woman was referring to her. "I'm Amelia. You can come with me," the small woman motioned for Lexy to follow.

"Oh, call me Lexy, please." She awkwardly requested, not wanting to explain that she was in fact not Mrs. Thompson. She was Miss Lexy Price. Truthfully, she loved hearing someone refer to her as Mrs. Thompson. She felt as if she could easily get used to that title.

While Amelia worked her magic on Lexy's tight muscles, Lexy daydreamed about being Mrs. Thompson. Though, the glaring truth was in the back of her mind. There already was a Mrs.

19

Thompson. The hour-long massage went by far too quickly, and Lexy was putting her robe back on before she knew it. Handing Amelia a generous tip, she thanked her, "I had no idea how badly I needed that. You are exceptionally talented. I can't thank you enough." For a moment, Lexy thought about hugging her masseuse, but she knew that would be weird.

Lexy headed back to her hotel room energized for her afternoon date with George. After a hot shower, Lexy took her time blow-drying her hair. She picked out a tight sundress that accentuated her large, natural breasts. The lavender color of the dress was a striking contrast to her tan skin and bright, blonde hair. She spun around for herself, admiring her figure in her mirror. She was the polar opposite of Penelope. Lexy was exciting, colorful, and sexy. Although Penelope was gorgeous, she had zero sex appeal. She was a missionary-only kind of woman. Lexy was convinced George was bored of his wife; Penelope was a flavorless stalk of celery compared to Lexy's juicy, ripe watermelon.

While Lexy was applying the final touches of her makeup, George returned from his morning meetings. "Well, hot damn! I might have to eat you for lunch." He tugged at her dress, willing her to take it off.

"George!" Lexy swatted his hand away. "I want

to explore! We can play later." She sprayed a spritz of perfume on her right wrist before slowly rubbing it against her left. "I thought we could check out Santa Monica. I've always wanted to walk on the pier!"

"Your wish is my command," George jokingly bowed. "I'll get an Uber to take us." George arranged the Uber driver while Lexy transferred a few important items from her purse to a small, woven clutch. "The driver is right around the corner. We can head down to the lobby whenever you're ready."

Lexy gave George a seductive kiss before walking out of the hotel room. "Today is going to be so much fun!" She clapped her hands together, unable to control her excitement. "Sorry, sorry. I know. Fit in, be calm." She straightened her dress then extended her hand to George, "Well, let's not keep the driver waiting."

As they walked through the hotel's lobby, Lexy could feel Jake's eyes on her. George must have noticed too; he draped his arm around her shoulders and pulled her close as they walked to the entrance. Lexy enjoyed seeing him squirm.

Their driver was polite and quiet, but Lexy could see the judgmental eyes watching them in the rearview mirror. George was seventeen years older than Lexy. Though, he was incredibly attractive for his age. He was in excellent shape with well-defined abs to show for it. He had thick, dark hair and dark eyes. As much of a head-turner as Lexy was, George turned a few heads as well.

"Do you have any suggestions for a lunch spot near the Santa Monica Pier?" Lexy asked the driver.

"There is a restaurant right on the pier called The Albright. It has some seafood and beer. It's pretty good." The driver seemed uninterested in furthering the conversation but suggested the restaurant to Lexy nonetheless. Not wanting to push for more information, George and Lexy decided they would eat lunch at The Albright.

Once they reached the pier, the excitement of being in California flooded over Lexy once more. She didn't travel very often, and she was thoroughly enjoying taking in the scenery of a different coast. They ventured down to the end of the pier before returning to the restaurant.

"We'd love to sit outside," George informed the young hostess at The Albright. She led them to a table with a bright, yellow umbrella.

"This is charming," Lexy said as she took in their surroundings. For the first time in years, she felt genuinely happy. She didn't feel like a single thing was missing.

"I think I'll have a beer if you are going to drink one," George hinted. Lexy never turned down a beer. She ordered an Angel City IPA, and George requested the Chihuahua Lager. They sipped their beers over an appetizer of the seasonal ceviche while they waited for their lunches. Their conversation started to diminish, but their matching orders of fish and chips showed up in the nick of time. With their mouths full, they set in silence, enjoying their meals.

"What do you want to do after this?" Lexy asked George once their plates were clear.

"I was thinking we could wander into Palisades Park. The views are pretty incredible. We can head in the direction of Montana Avenue." George had been to Santa Monica many times, whereas Lexy had never been. She wondered if he had ever been to Palisades Park with Penelope. She kicked the thought out of her head as soon as it entered. She was determined to enjoy her time with George; she hated thinking about his marriage. She only had so many minutes to spend with him. It was pointless to waste a single one on negative thoughts.

It was warm in Santa Monica, but unlike Charleston, the humidity wasn't a factor. There was a light breeze that brushed over their skin as they walked. Their conversation mainly revolved around their environment. It helped liven up their dialogue. They took turns pointing out people, trees, and viewpoints. They walked through Palisades Park for twenty minutes before reaching Montana Avenue. "I have a surprise for you," George announced.

"What is it?" Lexy asked, giddy to hear his response.

"Are you okay with walking for a bit longer? It's another mile or so, up Montana Avenue. We can have an Uber pick us up from there." Lexy nodded, grabbing hold of his hand once again. They ventured down the avenue together and wandered into a few stores along the way, admiring all that Montana Avenue had to offer. "We have arrived at the surprise location," George pointed to the Moondance Jewelry Gallery that was positioned directly in front of them. Lexy, simultaneously confused and delighted, gasped when she read the sign. A jewelry store. George had never purchased jewelry for her, although he had showered her with a few gifts during the beginning of their relationship.

As they browsed the jewelry selection, a ring caught George's eye. "That's the one," he pointed to a beautiful 14k rose gold ring with five graduating round bezel-set pink Sapphires. The sales associate pulled the ring out of the display case, offering it to Lexy to try on. She cautiously took the ring from the associate; she wasn't used to such nice things.

"It fits perfectly!" The ring slipped on her

finger as if it were designed specifically for her. Lowering her voice, Lexy whispered, "I don't know George. It's too much." She admired the ring on her finger, feeling ashamed for how badly she wanted it. George could see it in her eyes. She loved it.

"Nonsense. It's perfect for you. This will take care of it," he said, handing his payment to the associate. Lexy didn't know what to say. No one had ever been so generous to her. It wasn't even a special occasion! Lexy couldn't take her eyes off the ring during their Uber ride back to the hotel. Once they were alone in their room, Lexy showed George just how grateful she was.

Chapter 4

"I made dinner reservations right around the corner. It's a hip spot called 71Above. I requested the Sky Lounge; you'll be able to see every rooftop in Los Angeles while we dine." George announced to Lexy as she lied next to him in their hotel bed. He boasted about his plans; he knew his mistress was easily impressed.

Lexy bounced up and down on the bed like a schoolgirl. "That sounds so romantic!" She softly fell onto George's lap, kissing him. "I need to get ready!" The energy Lexy had was inspiring, but George also found it to be exhausting. He shut his eyes while she got ready for their night out.

"Okay, what do you think?" Lexy asked.

George opened his sleepy eyes to a spectacular view. Lexy's hair was pulled back into a tight bun. She had on a slim, black dress with a high neckline. Her strong shoulders were on display, and she looked fierce. There were many times in the past when she had made George's jaw drop, but this look floored him. She wasn't showing the usual bits and pieces he was used to, yet she grabbed his attention just the same.

"Well?" She asked once again, feeling insecure by his silence.

Teasing her, he rubbed his eyes before taking another look at her. "I've never seen you look more beautiful," he claimed. She blushed at his compliment. He took a quick shower and changed clothes before they headed out to their reservation.

When they arrived at The Sky Lounge, Lexy was overwhelmed by the view it offered of Los Angeles. George had good taste; everywhere he took Lexy delighted her. After their hostess led them to their reserved table, Lexy snuggled into George, taking in his masculine smell. She hoped that they looked like a real couple to the strangers around them.

Their meal consisted of three courses. First, they both started with the Burrata with Summer Squash. For their second courses, George ordered the Scallop Crudo and Lexy ordered the Duck Confit Terrine. The third course was decided by George. He ordered the Japanese Wagyu for the two of them. Every course was phenomenal. They worked their way through a bottle of wine, and when the waiter offered to open a second bottle, they obliged. They weren't encountering any awkward silences for once. The conversation flowed with the wine; the more they drank, the more they opened up.

"Would you ever leave your wife?" Lexy asked nonchalantly, pretending to review the dessert menu. As cool as she was trying to act, it had taken her all evening to work up the courage to ask him that question.

George chuckled, "I don't know. Possibly." He usually avoided discussing the future with Lexy, but he had already prepared for the conversation. "I honestly wish my wife would just – poof – disappear," he snapped his fingers. "Divorce is messy." He took another gulp of his wine, reaching for the bottle to refill his glass. "All I know is, if Penelope wasn't in the picture, I would be with you."

Those were the words Lexy had been dying to hear. It confirmed for her what she thought she knew all along. He felt stuck with Penelope. She could fix that! "Why don't we get rid of her then?"

"The only way to get rid of her would be to kill her. Otherwise, she would ruin me in a divorce." He said it very matter-of-fact. To Lexy, they had found their solution. Penelope needed to be cut out of the picture, and then Lexy could be with George. She could have him all to herself.

They finished their second bottle of wine before stumbling back to the hotel together. Waking up the next morning, neither of them was sure who fell asleep first. They had consumed far too much alcohol at dinner and had splitting headaches to prove it. "I had arranged for us to go on a hike to the Hollywood Sign, but I don't think I can muster up the strength," George said.

Lexy covered her mouth, running to the bathroom. She emerged a few minutes later. "Trust me, I don't want to do any hiking today," she explained. "Let's just hang out. We never get to do that." She got back into bed next to him.

Throughout the day, they only got out of bed a handful of times. They ordered dinner from a place in Chinatown that George had suggested called Howlin' Rays. He ordered The Sando, a Nashville hot chicken sandwich, for both of them. They ate their messy sandwiches in the crisp, white hotel sheets careful to not stain them. They bickered over what to watch, they playfully flirted, and they cuddled without it leading to sex. Their day spent lazily in bed made Lexy feel more at ease with George. She felt as if she was getting to know a different side of him, and it was a side she thoroughly enjoyed. That was the day Lexy decided she could spend her life with George.

Neither of them brought up the conversation they had the night before. Though, Lexy kept considering what he had said. He would be with her if Penelope wasn't in the picture. Was it that simple?

The morning after their hungover day spent

in bed, they woke up feeling like themselves again. It was their last full day in Los Angeles, and George had his final meetings. Out the door by nine, George's absence gave Lexy some alone time.

She made some coffee in the complimentary pot in the hotel room before calling her best friend, Nora, to update her on the trip. She told her every last detail, excluding the conversation she had with George the night before regarding Penelope. "Wait until you see the ring George bought me. It's insanely gorgeous!"

"I'm so glad to hear you're having a nice time! Do you still want me to pick you up from the airport tomorrow afternoon?" Nora asked. Lexy almost forgot; Nora was planning on picking her up so that George could head straight home to his wife. The thought of their trip ending, and George going back to his perfect life, made Lexy sick to her stomach. Lexy and Nora finalized their plans for the next afternoon and said their goodbyes. Lexy was grateful she had a friend like Nora.

The rest of the day, Lexy sulked in her hotel room. Although she was looking forward to spending the evening with George, the thought of it being their last night together couldn't escape her. She knew how their relationship – or lack of – was in Charleston.

Lexy started getting ready around the time George was due back to the hotel room. She didn't want to ruin the evening with her negative mind-set. After a shower and an attitude adjustment, she was thrilled to see George when he walked through the door.

"A colleague was telling me about the lobster roll he had at The Bunker Hill Bar & Grill. Would you be interested in going there? It's a casual atmosphere and right across the street." He was changing out his suit and tie for a polo shirt and shorts while she watched him closely. Already dressed in denim shorts and a halter top, a casual evening sounded perfect to Lexy.

They spotted The Bunker Hill the moment they stepped out of the hotel. Lexy rubbed her bare arms, and George swooped in to provide warmth. He might have been a cheating scoundrel, but at least he had the manners of a southern gentleman.

In celebration of the final evening of their trip, they both ordered cocktails. Lexy downed her drink with enthusiasm while George carefully sipped his. Already halfway into hers, Lexy finally had the courage she needed to speak up. "I was thinking about the conversation we had the other night," she said.

George rubbed his head and let out a deep, dramatic sigh. He was hoping she had forgotten all about their conversation. "We were wasted. I was venting, and you were humoring me. That's all it was. It meant nothing more. Please, drop it. Are you going to order the lobster roll as well?"

"Don't try to change the subject," she demanded. She had never spoken to George in that way, but she was annoyed that he was brushing her off so easily. Though, Lexy didn't want their last evening together to be tense. She immediately regretted her snappy response. "You're right. I'm sorry." Lexy brought the cocktail up to her lips, draining the rest of it. "You know, I would kill her for you. I could make it look like an accident or some shit." Although Lexy went out frequently, she never was good at handling her liquor.

George's face was unreadable. The waitress took their order before George finally spoke, "I would be devastated if anything were to happen to you. You could go to jail." His argument was rather emotionless and unconvincing. He expressed no concern for Penelope though which meant something to Lexy. Even if he meant nothing by it, she had already read into it.

They changed the subject and casually chatted throughout the rest of their meal. Once they made it back to their hotel room, their evening was spent between the sheets, making love and watching movies. They stayed up late, and both of them only caught a few hours of shuteye before they headed out for their flight.

George was preoccupied with his laptop

through most of the flight, and reality started to set in for Lexy. Their journey to California had been vastly different than the return trip. They were headed back to their separate lives, and George was preparing himself.

Once their plane touched the ground in Charleston, Penelope started texting George non-stop. It made Lexy feel jealous even though she knew it was silly to feel that way. After retrieving their luggage, George and Lexy went their separate ways. There was no goodbye kiss, just a short, friendly hug.

Lexy stepped out of the airport and was immediately greeted by a wave of humid air welcoming her back to her beloved town. In almost perfect timing, Nora pulled up in her white Toyota Corolla. She jumped out of the car and greeted her best friend. "I missed you so much!" Nora declared.

"I missed you more!" Lexy shrieked and squeezed Nora tightly. As much fun as it was to have George all to herself, Lexy loved her apartment, her space, and her best friend.

Once home, Lexy unlocked her apartment door and appreciated the familiar creak it made when she entered. As much as she loved traveling to California with George, she was equally pleased to be home.

Nora and Lexy made themselves comfortable on Lexy's couch. They spent the next couple of hours catching each other up. They rarely spent time apart, and they needed to divulge every little detail about their lives the other had missed over the week.

Lexy showed off the ring George had purchased for her, and Nora gushed over it. Although Nora thought the lavish gift from a married man was strange and inappropriate, she didn't want to shatter Lexy's illusions. Lexy was glowing with happiness, and that was good enough for Nora.

"It's Friday! Let's go out tonight!" Nora pleaded with Lexy. She was obviously grateful to have her partner in crime back in town. "I didn't do shit while you were gone."

Lexy pretended to consider her best friend's argument for a moment, but she knew she had no intention of leaving her apartment that evening. "I would love to, but I would be zero fun. You're more than welcome to stay here with me. We can watch Bravo and eat homemade nachos."

Nora shook her head, "Girl, I would love to. I haven't told you the full truth. I kind of made plans tonight, with that guy I hooked up with last week, Steve. From Tinder. I know, I know. I didn't even like him. Don't criticize me!" Although they took different routes, they both knew how to find the worst guys. Lexy didn't want Nora to go alone, but she couldn't muster up the energy. The thought of wearing clothes sounded nauseating to her. "I invited Mia, so I have someone coming with me at least. But she's not you."

Instantly, the guilt weighing Lexy down was lifted. Nora wouldn't be alone. She would be her wing-woman next time. Tonight, she was focusing on herself. Nora headed out for her evening plans, and Lexy climbed into her bathtub with a glass of wine.

Lexy repeatedly checked her phone. Although she knew better than to expect a text from George so soon, part of her hoped he would say something. After finishing nearly an entire bottle of wine, Lexy concluded that George wasn't going to text her, not yet anyway. Most likely, he was entertaining his wife and enjoying his gorgeous home. He wasn't thinking about Lexy.

Wine drunk and annoyed, Lexy turned to the internet. Feverishly typing into the search bar on her phone's internet browser, she hit enter. The search popped up with different links and suggestions. She scanned through them, unsure of what she was looking for. The bright light of her phone screen was irritating her eyes, and she tossed her phone off the side of her bed. Drifting off into a deep slumber, she dreamed she was back in Los Angeles with George.

Chapter 5

The next morning, Lexy woke to feelings of disappointment and nausea. Her mornings waking next to George were already a distant memory; she was alone once again. As much as she wanted to hide under the covers, her bladder forced her to get out of bed. She tripped over her unpacked suitcase on her way to the bathroom, cursing it. After relieving herself, she sat down on the floor next to the tightly-packed suitcase. Her favorite facial cleanser was still packed away, and she had forgotten to wash her face the night before. Lexy liked a heavy face of makeup, and she knew better than to leave it on overnight.

While the room felt like it was spinning, Lexy searched for the cleanser. Suddenly, she felt the sharp edge of paper cut the tip of her finger. "What the hell?" she said to herself while tugging at the mysterious piece of paper. She tried to remember what it could be. She considered that it could be a receipt, but she hadn't paid for a single thing in California.

She finally managed to free the piece of paper.

At first glance, she could tell it was ripped from the notepad in their hotel room. In George's messy handwriting, the note said, "I love you." Lexy's mouth filled with vomit, and she ran to the bathroom. Although she would probably tell Nora it was the culprit, the note wasn't what made her sick. The amount of alcohol she had the evening before did it to her.

Seeing the note did come as a shock to her though. George had said those words to her only one other time. To have them in writing, that was another thing. Maybe he did love her. She knew it was normal to not hear from him for a few days, especially after spending time together. She knew she needed to be patient, but it was difficult for her.

After a plate of scrambled eggs and a few glasses of water, Lexy was feeling better. Dressed in only a pair of panties and a tank top, she started straightening up her bedroom. Before she unpacked, she needed to at least minimize the clutter around her. Her packing process had been messy, to say the least, and clothes still covered the floor of her closet. As she hung up some items, tossing others into her laundry bin, her floor started to become visible again.

While unpacking, she came across the top she had worn the last evening in Los Angeles. Sauce from her lobster roll had dripped onto it creating a small stain. Knowing she was all out of stain remover, she retrieved her phone to search for a DIY method. Pulling up her internet browser, she was greeted with her search from the evening before. She let out a small gasp before quickly exiting the browser window. Her stomach clenched, and she once again felt nauseous. The evening before, in her drunken stupor, she had searched for ways to kill someone that you could stage as an accident. She felt like an idiot. She retrieved the note George had hidden in her suitcase and told herself that she wanted to help George. That's why she searched such a ludicrous thing. He was unhappy, and she was trying to help him. She was convinced that he truly loved her, not Penelope. Lexy knew that if Penelope was the one keeping them apart, she had to get rid of her.

Lexy spent the rest of the weekend doing chores, organizing her apartment, and preparing for her upcoming week back to work. When Monday morning came, it was harder than ever for Lexy to get out of bed. She imagined Penelope drinking coffee on her porch that overlooked the Charleston Harbor. Standing there in her dingy scrubs, she felt a sting of envy. Although the morning was rough, the workweek was off to a good start for Lexy. She genuinely enjoyed working as a nurse. Although she tended to be selfish in her personal life, oddly enough, she felt like her life calling was to help others.

Her normal annual patients came in for their check-ups along with a few new patients. She enjoyed chatting with them and hearing about their lives. The day was over before she knew it, and soon she was parking in front of her little apartment downtown. On her way inside, she noticed her overflowing mailbox. She retrieved the mail and kicked herself for not emptying it right when she got home from her trip.

Threatened by the large stack in front of her, Lexy poured a glass of wine to help her complete the task at hand. Letter by letter, she lowered the tall stack. More than half of the letters were junk mail. She found it infuriating that people could so easily solicit through the mail. She was wasting her time opening and tossing letters into the trash. Reaching for the next letter, she noticed there wasn't a return address on the envelope. She opened it to find a short, typed note. It read, "George manipulates his mistresses into killing his wives. He's done it before, and he's doing it again. You think you'll be his next wife, but you'll be his next victim."

Lexy read the letter over and over again. She couldn't believe what she was holding in her hands. Was it a warning? A threat? Grabbing the envelope again, she searched for some type of clue as to where the letter came from. How did someone know she had been contemplating killing George's wife? More importantly, how did someone know about her and George's relationship? Her heart started racing. Whoever it was, they knew where she lived. They had her address.

It did occur to her that the warning might be someone trying to help her. George had made it crystal clear he didn't want anything to happen to Penelope. He wasn't even trying to convince Lexy to kill her, at least not yet. Refilling her glass of wine, Lexy sat down with the letter. Hours passed by as she stared at it, willing it to tell her more.

She didn't finish opening the rest of her mail, and she forgot to eat dinner. Lexy's evening was ruined. She climbed into bed with an empty stomach and felt defeated. She knew she shouldn't have gotten involved with a married man, and someone had caught onto them. Someone knew their dirty little secret. The only person she had ever told about George was Nora. It crossed Lexy's mind that it was possible, though unlikely, that her best friend was the one behind the letter. Nora could have easily snuck it in her mailbox. She couldn't think of a logical reason why Nora would, though. As much as she detested George, Nora wouldn't sink that low.

Lexy tossed and turned all night, unable to get any real sleep. She felt uncomfortable in her apartment and was thrilled to return to work the next morning. The rest of the week, she kept a similar routine. She would work all day before going home to stare at the letter. She hadn't heard from George once since they said goodbye to each other at the airport. Even though they had gone days without talking before, it didn't sit well with Lexy's frantic mind.

She exchanged text messages with Nora throughout the week as they usually did. On Friday morning, Nora proposed a girls' night out for that night. Lexy hated that she felt suspicious of her best friend. Deep down, she knew Nora wasn't behind the letter, but she couldn't shake the accusation out of her head. She felt like she was starting to lose it, and the last thing she needed was a night out.

Lexy called Nora when she got off work that evening to explain herself. "I've had a shitty week," she said. "I honestly don't feel like going out and getting hit on by random creeps tonight. Let's have a beach day tomorrow though! I could use some vitamin D."

"You're getting lame in your old age," Nora teased her. She was used to Lexy wanting to go out every weekend. Nora had noticed a change in her ever since she started seeing George, but she knew there was nothing she could do about it. Lexy was a grown woman. "The beach sounds perfect though. Come over to my place tomorrow morning around ten?" The two usually inseparable women hadn't spent much time together recently, and Nora was eager to see her best friend.

"I might be there a little before ten if that's okay. I haven't been able to sleep very well lately. I'm restless." Lexy slyly hinted that something was off with her, but she didn't want to go into detail over the phone. She wanted to talk to Nora about the letter in person. It's not as if she was truly suspecting Nora was behind the letter. Lexy knew her better than that. After contemplating all week, she had finally concluded that the person who sent it was most likely someone that used to work in the same department as them at the hospital. It was the only rational assumption she could make.

Nora didn't press for more information. "You know you're welcome over here whenever," she told Lexy. "I'll see you tomorrow!"

With a beach day to look forward to the following day, Lexy tried to relax on her Friday evening. She watched old reruns of The O.C. and ordered Chinese food, successfully distracting herself for a few hours. She considered texting George, just to say she hoped he had a good week. She knew that was stupid though. He would have contacted her if he wanted to. For the first night that week, she drifted off to sleep early.

Lexy woke in the middle of the night startled; a loud thumping noise was coming from her front door. Shaking in fear, she waited to see if anyone would attempt to enter her apartment. She knew they wouldn't be able to; the door had a double deadbolt. A few moments later, she heard giggling. Lexy made her way in the dark over to her door's peephole and looked out. She saw two college-aged girls, tripping over each other. She recognized one as her neighbor and realized the two drunk idiots were behind the mysterious thuds. Lexy felt both annoyed and embarrassed; her imagination was starting to run wild. In the silence of her bedroom, she realized just how much the letter was already getting to her. Her paranoia would soon be too much for her to handle; she needed answers.

Chapter 6

Golden light danced into Lexy's room shortly after sunrise. It was a beautiful day without a cloud in sight. Lexy took a quick shower to shave her legs; something she had meant to do the night before. Lexy decided to wear her favorite gold bikini. It was a barely-there, string style bikini that displayed her perfectly toned body. She loved wearing a teeny bikini; more exposed skin meant more eyes on her. If there was one thing that could perk her up, it was a little extra attention.

Lexy was ready for her day and already out the door by nine. Nora's Isle of Palms condo was a twenty-minute drive from downtown, give or take. Seeing as it was still breakfast menu hours, Lexy decided to swing by Chick-fil-A to surprise Nora. Chick-n-Minis were a staple in Lexy and Nora's diets; it would hit the spot before a day drinking on the beach.

Nora was anticipating Lexy's arrival and left her front door unlocked. When Lexy entered with a Chick-fil-A bag, Nora applauded her. "That's what I'm talking about! Thanks, girl!" They ate their breakfast on Nora's porch. With a birds-eye view of the beach, they surveyed where they would post up for the day. There weren't too many beachgoers yet so their options were plentiful. It was one of the perks of getting to the beach early.

With a spot carefully selected, Nora and Lexy took their beach chairs down to the water-line. The tide was going out so they didn't have to worry about periodically moving their chairs back. Nora slathered her legs in tinted tanning oil before handing the bottle over to Lexy so that she could do the same. Aside from a couple of families already out with their kids, the two women had the beach to themselves.

Once they were relaxed, lounging in their chairs, Lexy thought it was time to open up to Nora about her unbelievable week. "I need to tell you something," she said to her friend. She looked away but could feel Nora staring at her.

"You're worrying me. What's wrong? Are you pregnant?" Nora questioned. Lexy playfully smacked Nora's shoulder and shook her head. Nora let out a huge sigh of relief in response. "Thank God. So what is it?" she asked.

Lexy dove right in, "I received an anonymous letter this week." She paused. "It basically said that George is a manipulative murderer. Honestly, it sounds ludicrous." Lexy was emotionless as she spoke. Nora's freckled face contorted into a look of shock and disgust. She waited for Lexy to continue. "It said that he was going to convince me to kill his wife and that I would be the next victim in line after her. It's probably a prank, don't you think?" Nora hadn't liked George ever since the first time Lexy told her about him; she had a bad feeling from the start.

Lexy was assured by Nora's reaction that she had nothing to do with the mysterious letter. Once again, she found herself feeling guilty for even considering such a thing. It was a hard week though, and her emotions had gotten the best of her. She should have known better than to suspect Nora, though. Her friend finally spoke, "Are you serious, Lexy?" Her voice was shaking. "You need to report that to the police. This isn't funny."

"No!" Lexy screamed and a family nearby looked in their direction. The mother of the family glared at the two of them. More times than not, women they encountered looked at them as if they were social lepers. Nora and Lexy knew these actions stemmed from jealousy, and it didn't bother them one bit. Lexy lowered her voice; she did not want to attract any unnecessary attention. Their conversation was extremely private and needed to remain that way. "I can't tell anyone! His wife would find out about everything. He would hate me."

"I think it would be better off having him hate

you than somehow you falling victim to whatever game he is playing. You have to stop seeing him! If you don't want to take this to the police, that is your decision, but you have to promise me you aren't going to see him anymore. It's not worth it!" Nora made a fair point, and Lexy knew she was right.

Lexy had been involved with plenty of men like George in the past, and she knew there would be many others in the future. For some reason, she wasn't ready to let go of George just yet, no matter what the letter said. She would appease her best friend for the time being. "I have no plans to see him," she promised Nora. "We haven't even talked since the airport, and I think that's for the best." It wasn't exactly a lie; she truly hadn't spoken to him since then. That wasn't her decision though.

As they were wrapping up their conversation about George, a football landed a couple of feet away from them. An attractive guy jogged over to retrieve it. He effortlessly tossed it back in the direction of his two friends before turning to greet them, "Hey ladies!"

Nora waved at him in response, and he took off running back in the direction of his friends. "He's hot," she giggled. Lexy nodded in agreement, but she hadn't heard what Nora said. She was still thinking about George and the letter.

The clock was inching closer to noon, and the

two women decided it was time for a beach cocktail. Technically, they weren't allowed to drink on the beach on Isle of Palms, but that rule had never stopped them in the past. After a quick trip to Nora's condo, they snuck their cocktails back onto the beach in Yeti Tumbler's.

The three guys were still tossing their football around, and the women enjoyed judging them from a distance. They were all athletic guys, and their bodies looked like they had been carefully sculpted. "Cheers to a damn good view," Nora said to Lexy.

Every so often, the guys would strategically throw their ball in Lexy and Nora's direction. The guys would take turns running over to retrieve it, casually striking up a conversation with the women every time. Eventually, Nora and Lexy had learned all three of their names: Elliot, Preston, and Wyatt.

All five of them ended up hanging out, and they enjoyed the rest of the afternoon as a group. Elliot and Wyatt were twins, and Preston was their best friend. They were visiting Charleston from Charlotte, North Carolina, and they were headed back home the following day.

Wrapping up the beach day, the guys invited Nora and Lexy to hang out with them that night. "We're just going to be taking it easy. We'll be staying in, but we'll toss back a few drinks. Do y'all want to come over to our place?"

Lexy wasn't in the mood to entertain men that evening, but she could tell by the look on Nora's face that she wouldn't hear the end of it if she said no. The guys had been fun all day. What harm could it do to hang out with them that night? Their condo was in the same building as Nora's so at least it was convenient. Nora had made plenty of sacrifices for her in the past, and it was Lexy's turn that night.

She let Nora answer for the two of them. "That sounds fun!" Nora sounded overly enthusiastic, and Lexy wished she had toned it down a bit. "We'll go get ready at my place then head over." They packed up their chairs and towels before re-treating to Nora's condo.

"I didn't bring anything extra to wear," Lexy complained. She wore the same size as Nora, and she knew it was a pathetically weak excuse. She did have her makeup with her; she always had it with her. She hated how she looked barefaced and wouldn't risk being caught without it.

Nora grabbed her hand and pulled her into her walk-in closet. She selected a cobalt blue halter top and a pair of denim shorts, handing them to Lexy, "The shorts are yours. I borrowed them last week while you were out of town and forgot to re-turn them. The top is yours too. I don't know how long I've had it. Sorry, I'm a bitch and don't return clothes. On the bright side, now you have something to wear!"

"I guess I'll just go braless and commando," Lexy joked. Nora already knew that was the norm for Lexy. "At least they are my shorts."

Nora's condo had a master bedroom and bathroom as well as a guest bedroom and bathroom. Lexy showered and got ready in the guest while Nora used the master. Emerging as brand new people, they complimented each other's looks. They never felt competitive with one another; they knew they both had a lot to offer.

The guy's condo was a few floors down from Nora's, and they talked about which guy they thought was the hottest on their way. "I like the shorter, bulkier guy. Wyatt? He is cute," Nora admitted.

Lexy had thought Wyatt was the nicest seeming of the three guys but made a mental note to stay away from him. Her best friend had already made her claim. She wasn't interested in any of the guys anyway; she was only going as a wing-woman for Nora. "Wyatt is cool. I like his style."

"Plus, he'll be gone tomorrow," Nora looked thrilled, and Lexy couldn't help but laugh. "You know I hate when guys get attached." She had commitment issues; an unavailable guy from out of town was exactly what Nora was looking for.

The guys answered the door with wide smiles and showed the girls inside. They were renting an Airbnb, and the three-bedroom condo was covered in beach décor. From the large, wooden anchor hanging on the wall to the shell knobs on the cabinets, every inch of the apartment was either coastal or nautical. It was tacky and made Nora appreciate the subtle décor in her own condo.

The guys challenged them to a game of beer pong, and they agreed to play guys against girls. The girls had no trouble defeating the guys. Wyatt was especially impressed with Nora, and they flirted throughout the night. Lexy was happy for her friend, but she couldn't get George off of her mind. Around midnight, she decided to send him a text message. It said, "I need to see you."

Chapter 7

George was in bed with Penelope when he received a text message from his mistress. He glanced over at his peaceful wife; she was fast asleep. Less than a minute after receiving the message, George responded informing Lexy that he would be at her place within an hour. Penelope was used to George leaving in the middle of the night; it wasn't suspicious with his career. He woke her up to say goodbye, and she groggily told him that she loved him before he headed out into the night.

Lexy wasn't expecting such a quick response from George, and she panicked when she realized she didn't have much time to get home. "I'm not feeling so great," she told Nora. "I think I need to head home."

"Why don't you go back to my place and sleep in the guest bedroom, like we planned? You don't need to go all the way back home tonight. Plus, you've been drinking." As hard as Nora tried, there was no convincing Lexy. She had a one-track mind at that point; she wanted to see George, and she was relieved that he wanted to see her as well. Nothing was going to stop her.

"I already requested an Uber ride. Are we still on for lunch downtown tomorrow?" Lexy asked. "Maybe I can catch a ride back here with you afterward to get my car." Nora kept giving Lexy a look, a look that said that she knew what she was up to, but she didn't say anything more. She reluctantly agreed that the plans for Sunday would work before Lexy headed out.

Lexy got back to her apartment only seconds before George pulled up himself. "Where is your car?" He asked her. George didn't hug her or approach her.

"It's on Isle of Palms. I spent the day with Nora out there," she answered him very matter-of-fact. She felt uncomfortable by the way he was acting, but she tried not to show it. She unlocked her door, and they stepped inside. The second they were alone in the dark, George's hands grabbed her face and brought her lips to his. She was caught off guard, but responded quickly, and wrestled with his belt. While undressing her married lover, Lexy remembered the letter she had received. She immediately pulled away from George and turned on her living room lamp.

"What's wrong?" He started to rub her shoulders, and his grip was firmer than she was used to. "I thought you would be excited to see me.

I'm sorry I didn't call you all week. Work was crazy." Lexy didn't know if there was any truth behind the letter, but it creeped her out nonetheless. When she sent George a text message that night, she had no intention of winding up back at her place with him. She had missed him though, and his hands felt good on her sunkissed shoulders.

"I am excited to see you," she explained. "It's been a long day; I'm tired." He worked his way from her shoulders down to her lower back, caressing the bare skin between her shorts and halter top. She knew what he wanted, and she couldn't help herself. She gave in.

"I need to head out," George announced a few minutes after they had finished their extramarital activities. "My wife thinks I've been at the hospital, but my shift starts in thirty. I need to go get changed."

"You can change here," Lexy offered. George shook his head, denying her offer. He didn't explain why, but Lexy knew he didn't want to be seen taking a bag inside her apartment. He was neurotic anytime he came over. The college students that lived around Lexy didn't pay any attention to them, but that didn't matter to George. He had a guilty conscience, and he was paranoid. "When will I see you again?" Lexy asked. She regretted how needy the question came off, but it was already out there.

"I don't know Lexy. I'll sneak over here before or after shifts if I can, I promise." He kissed her forehead and left her apartment. She had so much she wanted to say to him, but he didn't even give her the chance. He ran their relationship; she was at his mercy. It was a weak, pathetic position to be in, and she hated it.

It was almost two in the morning by that point, and Lexy was hungry. She searched her kitchen for something edible, landing on a frozen pizza. While the pizza cooked in the oven, Lexy thought about Nora. She shouldn't have left her alone with three strangers. It was probably too late to get a response, but Lexy sent a text to check on her. A couple of minutes later, Nora responded with an eggplant emoji. At least one of them was having a good night. Lexy's pizza was the best thing about her night. She settled into bed around four, closing her curtains to guarantee the sun wouldn't wake her too soon.

Lexy's loud ringtone startled her at some point in the morning; she forgot to put her phone on silent. "What?" She groaned into the phone.

"Good morning, beautiful!" Nora sounded energetic, too energetic for Lexy.

"What time is it?" Lexy asked.

"It's almost noon. I'm in my car headed to your place. Get up!" Lexy didn't budge, and she had no plans to. "You're going to want your car for work tomorrow, you know. We don't have to go to lunch." Lexy let out a sigh of relief.

Nora had a key to Lexy's apartment and let herself right in. Her friend was tucked under her covers, fast asleep. With Lexy still in bed, Nora poked around. She was looking for any evidence that George had been there the night before. To her disappointment, she couldn't find any. "Wake up, sleepyhead," Nora pulled the curtains open, allowing natural light to flood into Lexy's bedroom. "Wyatt is taking me to the beach at three so we need to get moving!"

"I take it things went well with him last night? You can't stop smiling," Lexy forced enthusiasm for her best friend. She was genuinely excited for her, but her excitement was clouded by her frustration with George. She regretted leaving Isle of Palms the night before to see him; it wasn't worth it. She should have stayed with Nora.

"He's already made it to the top five," Nora bragged. As long as Lexy had known her, Nora had kept a list rating the men she slept with. It was one of Lexy's favorite things about her best friend. It was a hilarious habit, and she enjoyed hearing her ratings.

"Ever?!" Lexy gasped.

"Ever. It was that good. He's driving back to

Charlotte later this afternoon, but he wants to go on a walk on the beach with me first." Lexy thought it sounded cliché, but it was nice to see Nora happy. "He says he wants to come here to visit me on the weekends. At first, it freaked me out, but I kind of like the idea of it."

"Okay, what have you done with my best friend? You can't spend your weekends with a boy toy! I need you," Lexy whined. She was finally out of bed and putting clothes on. "Well, let's get you to your new man." She knew Nora would be over her crush in a matter of hours.

Once Lexy was dressed and her teeth were brushed, Nora pushed her out the front door. During the drive to Isle of Palms, Nora's mouth moved a mile a minute, divulging every last detail from her evening with Wyatt. Lexy was only partially listening, but she got the gist of it. Once they reached Nora's place, Lexy got right into her Ford Mustang convertible and turned around to head home.

Rather than take the Isle of Palms Connector, the bridge that connects the town of Mount Pleasant to Isle of Palms, Lexy drove the scenic route with her convertible top down. She took Palm Boulevard to Breach Inlet then continued on Jasper Boulevard until she reached the Ben Sawyer Bridge. Lexy preferred this route home. Luckily, the swing bridge wasn't open and she was able to drive right over the Ben Sawyer Bridge. Admiring the marsh around her, she spotted the Old Village. She thought of George and Penelope. On a whim, she decided to drive by their house. No one was home, and she stopped in front of the driveway to admire their gorgeous house. It was risky; Penelope could pull up at any moment. Lexy drove away, watching the house in her rearview mirror. She wanted to see inside of it. Better yet, she wanted to live in it.

For the rest of the afternoon and into the evening, Lexy lounged around her apartment, staring at the letter. She barely got any chores done before nighttime crept up on her.

Lexy was unprepared for Monday morning when it rolled around. The letter was all she could think about; she was obsessing over it. When she first received it, she was convinced it wasn't true, but as time went on, she started to reconsider it. George could be capable of anything, how well did she even know him? She was only as close to him as he let her be.

By midweek, Lexy was able to focus again at work, and she was much more productive because of it. After lunch, a new patient came in for a physical and blood work. Before the doctor saw a new patient, it was Lexy's job to get their medical history and their vital signs.

"Rutledge Campbell?" Lexy called out in the

waiting room. A tall man stood up. He had bright blue eyes that matched the sky. Lexy immediately took notice of how attractive he was.

"Yes ma'am," he said in response, walking towards Lexy. He followed her to the exam room, and she could feel his eyes on her body.

While they were chatting about Rutledge's medical history, they wound up on the topic of his occupation. "I'm a private investigator. It's mainly local work, but I do a couple of out of town gigs a year," he explained to her. Lexy was fascinated. She felt as if it was fate that they crossed paths; she could use the help of a private investigator. She didn't want to get into the details at work though; it wasn't the time or place.

"Would you mind if I got a business card from you?" Lexy asked him. "I actually might be able to use your services." From the look on his face, Rutledge thought she meant something else. He quickly got his card out and handed it to her. She finished reviewing his medical history and told him she would be in touch. As much as she wanted to hang around, she had to retrieve her next patient.

Later that evening, Lexy dialed the phone number listed on Rutledge's business card. "Hello?" A deep voice with a southern accent answered.

"Rutledge? This is Lexy, your nurse from this afternoon." Her voice trembled as she spoke. As much as she wanted his help, she was afraid to ask for it.

"How can I help you, Lexy?" His friendly response made her feel more at ease. Plus, she liked the way he said her name.

"I have a business proposal for you," she announced. "Would you like to meet me for dinner tomorrow night?" Lexy even surprised herself by how professional she sounded.

There was a long pause on the other end of the line. "If we're going to be discussing something private, we need to meet somewhere private. Let's meet on the beach. Sullivan's Island. Station 18. Be there at seven tomorrow evening," he commanded. Lexy assumed he knew what he was talking about and agreed to meet him.

Chapter 8

Thursday moved in slow motion for Lexy. She was anxious for her meeting with Rutledge, and seven o'clock couldn't come soon enough. Instead of driving back to her apartment downtown after work, she decided to stay in Mount Pleasant and grab a drink until it was time to meet him. She didn't want to fight the traffic on the Arthur Ravenel Jr. Bridge twice.

After two beers, Lexy made the smart decision to switch to water and ordered an appetizer. An older man tried to start a conversation with her, but she made it obvious she wasn't interested. She was trying to focus before her conversation with Rutledge. She wanted to be prepared. Finally, it was a quarter to seven, and it was time for Lexy to head to Sullivan's Island.

The alcohol did nothing for her nerves, and her stomach felt tense. She drove over the Ben Sawyer Bridge and turned right onto Middle Street. It was a beautiful night, and the small strip of restaurants on Sullivan's Island was packed. Making her way to Station 18, she contemplated turning around. Lexy could easily park her car, order a Gamechanger at Home Team BBQ, and forget the whole thing. Sharing the letter with a stranger was dangerous. It was stupid. She knew better, yet she was on her way to meet him anyway.

Once Lexy turned onto Station 18, she easily found a parking spot along the side of the road. She waited in her car until her clock hit seven on the dot. She tucked the anonymous letter underneath her driver seat and got out on shaky legs.

"Miss Lexy!" The voice behind her made her jump. She turned around to see Rutledge getting out of an older Chevy Tahoe that was parked directly behind her Mustang. She wasn't the least bit surprised by his choice of transportation. He must have pulled up right after her; she hadn't noticed.

"Thanks for meeting me here," Lexy tried to act cool, but he had startled her. She started to walk towards the beach access, and Rutledge paused for a moment before following behind her. Lexy hoped he would catch up to her, but he lingered behind her. She slowed her pace to match his. "So, do we starting talk now? Do we wait? How does this work?" She asked as they walked together along the path that led to the beach.

"We wait," Rutledge found her questioning humorous. "We're almost to the safe zone." Sunset was only an hour away; the golden hour was in full force. The lighting brought out Rutledge's features; the lines in his face gave him character. He was ruggedly handsome, and Lexy found herself staring at him. He abruptly stopped walking, and Lexy almost ran into him. "Here we are," he announced as he spread out a blanket and motioned for Lexy to take a seat on it.

Lexy hadn't even noticed he was carrying a blanket; she had been too busy admiring his features. She hadn't felt this fascinated by a man since the first time she met George. "Good thinking," was all she could manage to say. She was back to feeling nervous. She considered putting a move on Rutledge rather than divulging the truth about why she arranged their meeting. She wanted to jump his bones, and it would be a good excuse to avoid any discussion about the letter.

"This isn't my first rodeo," Rutledge said as he sat down across from her. "Whatever you tell me here tonight will stay between us. I give you my word." Lexy looked skeptical, but in reality, she was still trying to decide what she should do. Rutledge could sense that she was unsure, and he continued to sell himself. "I have a long list of secrets I've kept, and trust me, I forget things over time. I can't remember it all."

"I received an anonymous letter. It's pretty messed up. I don't know if I'm ready to share what it said with you, but I have a few questions about it. If you're willing to answer them without more information, I would be grateful," Lexy vaguely explained.

"I'm willing." Rutledge looked interested. After all, it was what he did for a living. He knew more Charleston secrets than Lexy could ever imagine. Lexy's secret was nothing compared to what he had seen and heard before.

"Is it possible to find out who sent the letter?" she asked. "It was typed, sent with no return address, and there were no unique markings on the envelope or letter."

Rutledge looked impressed. "Do you work as a detective on the side?" he kidded. "It's not impossible to find out, but with nothing to go off of, it's rather unlikely."

Satisfied with his answer, Lexy proceeded with her next question. "Is it possible to find out if there is any truth behind the letter?" she asked. "The message is a warning for me regarding a man I have been seeing."

"I'm disappointed to hear you're seeing someone," he confessed. Lexy blushed; they had an obvious unresolved sexual attraction towards one another. Under the circumstances, the flirting seemed inappropriate though. "I could certainly investigate the truth behind the claim," Rutledge returned to the subject. "I would need to know the details of the letter, and that includes the name of the mystery man."

Lexy motioned for Rutledge to move closer, and he did. "Can I trust you?" she whispered in his ear. He nodded in response, but neither of them moved a muscle. They both considered making a move on the other, but neither one did. "This isn't word for word, but the note said, 'George is going to trick you into killing his wife. He's done it before, and you'll be his next victim' or something like that," she disclosed to him before she pulled away.

"Well, damn," Rutledge looked befuddled. "That's a doozy. I can easily look into his martial history and see if there is any truth behind the claim. You will have to tell me his last name though."

Lexy was relieved that Rutledge didn't insist on seeing the letter. "It's Thompson," she murmured.

"George Thompson," Rutledge repeated. His voice was deep and carried.

"Be quiet!" Lexy covered his mouth with her hand, and she once again thought about kissing him. She quickly moved away and stood up. She brushed off the sand that had made its way onto her scrubs. "I need to head home," she announced. "When do you think you can get started on this?"

Rutledge gathered the blanket and folded it neatly. "I'll look into it first thing tomorrow morning," he assured her. Lexy somehow already felt comfortable with Rutledge, and she didn't trust people easily. She was relieved that their meeting had gone so well. They walked back to their cars together. "I'll be in touch tomorrow," Rutledge gave her his word.

"Wait, we didn't talk about your fee," Lexy said in a hushed voice. She had no idea what the going rate was for a private investigator.

"We'll work something out; don't worry about it," Rutledge said before climbing into his Tahoe. She liked the way he looked in it. She might have to do a little investigating herself; she was intrigued by him.

When she was only a few minutes away from her apartment, a text message from George came through on Lexy's phone. The message said, "Mind if I swing by?" Another booty call, she assumed. Although Lexy knew most affairs were made up primarily of booty calls, she naively thought that what she had with George was different.

Even after receiving the letter, she still couldn't say no to him. She wanted to see him more than anything, even if it was only for a quickie. She didn't care if he was using her; she needed the attention. She waited until she walked in her door before sending him a response. Although she was still somewhat reluctant, she told him to come by whenever. She realized she was still in her scrubs and quickly changed into satin shorts and a matching camisole. Not ten minutes after she arrived home, George was knocking on her door. He was gone as quickly as he came. They exchanged only a few words the entire time he was there; their bodies did most of the talking. Lexy couldn't help but think the letter had it all wrong. George had no interest in making Lexy his next wife. He was plenty happy having her as a side dish before going home to the main dish, Penelope.

Lexy heated a frozen dinner and plopped down on her couch with it. She flipped channels before she landed on the inevitable, Bravo. She ate her dinner while not listening to a word that was said on the television. Her mind was fixated on George; she regretted letting him use her that evening. She felt weak. She turned off the television and headed to her bathroom. After a hot bubble bath and a glass of wine, Lexy was ready for bed. Crawling under her covers, she wondered what Rutledge would find out about George. Her mind began to wander; she wanted to know more about the mysterious private investigator. Opening the Facebook app on her cell phone, she typed his name into the search bar. Nothing came up. She searched on Instagram and Twitter as well with no luck. Who the hell was Rutledge?

Her attention returned back to George and the letter. She suddenly remembered that she had stashed it under her driver's seat and rushed out to her car to retrieve it. She couldn't risk losing it or having someone find it; she needed to keep it safe. Once she had it in her hands, she studied it. Every time she looked over it, she hoped she would find a clue she had missed. She eventually dozed off, but even her dreams involved the letter.

She woke up the next day with heightened anxiety and a headache. She couldn't decide if she made the right decision the evening before. Sharing something so private with a stranger was out of character for her. Between the meeting with Rutledge and her visit from George, Lexy's evening had been eventful. No matter how many hours of sleep she had gotten, she felt exhausted at work. The letter was quickly wearing her down.

Chapter 9

While Lexy was on her lunch break, she received the obligatory Friday text message from Nora inquiring about her plans for the weekend. While Lexy was typing out a response to her, her phone started to ring. Rutledge Campbell's name came up on the screen. Lexy swallowed the rest of the sandwich bite that was in her mouth. "Hello?" she finally managed to say.

"Miss Lexy, it's Rutledge," he said politely. Every time Rutledge called Lexy 'miss', she wanted to jump his bones a little bit more.

"How are you?" Lexy asked. She didn't know if it was a positive or negative thing that she was already hearing from him. Her gut feeling told her Rutledge had already found something out about George.

Rutledge cleared his throat, "I'm good, thanks for asking. I found something that I wanted to discuss with you. Are you comfortable talking about it over the phone? I can be discreet with my words."

"Sure, that's fine," she responded. She was anything but fine. Her palms felt slippery against the phone. Her heart was racing; she wanted him to spit it out.

"He has been married before. Both of his previous wives died, and both deaths were ruled as accidents. One of his wives was the victim of a fire at their residence, started by a candle, and the other drowned in their pool while he wasn't home." Lexy couldn't believe what Rutledge was telling her. The letter did have some truth to it; she felt like a fool.

"How is that possible?" She knew it was a pointless question to ask. Rutledge knew no more than she did. "I thought his current wife was his first – and only – wife." The truth was, she didn't know George nearly as well as she thought she did. She had fallen into his trap. Whoever sent the letter was genuinely trying to help her.

Rutledge could hear the disappointment in Lexy's voice. He had more information to share with her, but he decided to wait. She had enough information to digest for the time being. "Would you like to get dinner with me tonight?" he requested. "We can talk more about this in person."

Lexy groaned, "I'm not in the mood to go anywhere tonight." She had already been in a bad mood all day, and after hearing what Rutledge had found out about George, she couldn't imagine going out to dinner. "Could you come over to my place instead? I know we just met, but I would feel more comfortable if we talked about all of this in the privacy of my home." She had ulterior motives, but she hoped it wasn't too obvious. At that point, she was pissed at George and was ready to get to know Rutledge on a deeper level.

"That sounds good. We will want some privacy for the thing we need to discuss. There is something else I found out about George that I need to tell you later," Rutledge wanted to prepare her. By that point, Lexy wasn't surprised to learn that there was more. She was slowly realizing that George wasn't the man she thought he was.

When she really thought about it, it all made sense to her. Motivated by what he had said in Los Angeles, Lexy had searched the internet for ways to kill someone while staging it like an accident. He had been so close to convincing her, and she hadn't even noticed. As much as she didn't want to admit it, she truly had considered killing George's wife. Whatever else Rutledge had to tell her, she was ready for it. "I'll text you my address," she told him. "I'll be home around six; feel free to come by anytime after that." She hung up the phone and immediately sent Rutledge her address. If she was going to have a rebound, Rutledge was the perfect guy for the job.

She deleted the text she had been typing to

Nora and instead explained to her that she had plans that evening. Before sending it, Lexy added that she promised they would catch up soon. She wished she could tell Nora everything that had been going on with George, and Rutledge, but she knew her best friend wouldn't understand. She didn't even fully understand it all herself.

Lexy felt perturbed the rest of the afternoon. She hid her phone in her purse in an attempt to avoid it for the rest of the day. When she went to retrieve it before heading home, she was greeted by two text messages and a missed phone call. They were all from George. Lexy's mind immediately went to the worst-case scenario: George somehow found out that she hired a private investigator to look into him.

When she opened the text messages, the contents were not what she was expecting. The messages told her that he was free that night, for a couple of hours, and wanted to see her. He promised he would be with her longer than a quickie and apologized for their last encounter. George wasn't one to apologize or admit any wrongdoing, so Lexy was taken aback by the message. Part of her wanted to call Rutledge, cancel their plans, and see her beloved George.

Suddenly, she remembered what Rutledge had told her. She remembered the letter. She sent George a short message back that said, "Can't.

Have plans with Nora. I'll let you make it up to me soon." A few minutes after she responded to George, he tried to call her. She let it go to voice-mail; she would let him think she was already with Nora. He didn't leave a message, and he didn't try to call again. Lexy felt both disappointed and relieved. Unfortunately, she still had strong feelings for George, no matter what she had learned about him that day. That wasn't something she could erase overnight.

Focusing on the evening ahead of her, and Rutledge, Lexy took a quick shower to freshen up. She put a white cotton t-shirt dress over her head, careful not to rub the fabric against her made-up face. The dress was thin and clung to her body; she felt casual but sexy in it. She had left her hair in a bun when she showered, not wanting to get it wet, and she readjusted it into a high ponytail.

The ring George gifted her grabbed her attention as it sparkled on her dresser. She had only taken it off to shower, but it didn't feel right to put it back on. The ring felt tainted. As beautiful as it was, what it represented was ugly. She placed it in a box and hid it in the back of her lingerie drawer.

Lexy's cooking skills were minimal, but she wanted to have something to offer Rutledge. She had already stopped by Trader Joe's on her way home from work for cheese, crackers, and an assortment of fruit. She assumed Rutledge was more of a meat-and-potatoes kind of guy, but she knew from experience that those guys typically loved cheese as well. She grabbed a few bottles of wine and some beer for beverage options; it would hopefully help lighten the mood.

While she was creating an amateur cheese plate, Rutledge sent her a text to let her know he was on his way. With this information, Lexy ran to the bathroom to check her makeup and apply any necessary touch-ups. Not long after she received his text, she heard a knock at her door. She was busy applying lip gloss and threw the tube down to go answer it. She looked out the peephole to double-check that it was who she was expecting. Rutledge was standing there with a bottle of wine in hand. She opened the door and invited him in.

"I forgot to mention that I live right down the street," he apologized.

Lexy had been caught off guard by his quick arrival, but she tried to play it cool, "No worries, I was just hanging out. Should we go ahead and pop that sucker open?" She pointed to the bottle in his hand. Before he could answer, she grabbed it out of his hand and headed towards her kitchen. Pulling out two glasses, she generously filled them.

"Good thinking. You might want to finish your glass before we start talking," Rutledge said as he reached for one of the glasses.

"Great," Lexy took a gulp. Whatever Rutledge had to tell her, it didn't sound good. "Go ahead and tell me. I can handle it." After another gulp, she looked towards Rutledge. "Well?"

He took a sip of his wine and looked around Lexy's apartment. "Interesting place you got here. It's very - pink." Her walls were white, but most of the artwork that hung on them was a shade of pink. Her throw pillows were pink, and the curtains were pink. It almost looked like a bottle of Pepto-Bismol had exploded inside of her apartment, turning it different shades of pink.

"It's my favorite color," she announced as if the overuse of the color didn't make her statement obvious enough.

"You don't say," Rutledge said as he winked at her. They both were controlling their natural urges. You could cut the sexual tension in the room with a knife. Rutledge had come to her apartment for business though, and they needed to focus on the business discussion before anything else could happen. "If you think you are ready to hear what I have to say, I will go ahead and tell you," he said.

Lexy refilled her glass, "I'm as ready as I'll ever be."

Chapter 10

Rutledge paused for a moment before bluntly explaining what he had learned about George. "Mr. Thompson already has another female friend," he told her. "The next in line has already been chosen." He pulled a photograph out of the folder he brought inside with him. The photo clearly showed an unknown redhead kissing George in a parking garage downtown. That's exactly where Lexy used to hook up with George, during the beginning of their relationship.

Lexy pulled the photo closer in an attempt to make out who the woman was, but all she could see was that she was wearing scrubs. Her face wasn't visible. For all she knew, it could be one of her old colleagues. She felt sick.

"Where did you get this?" Lexy asked. "Is this recent?"

Rutledge placed a hand on her leg. "I took it," he explained. "It's from earlier today. I'm so sorry, Lexy. After our phone conversation this morning, I wanted to go snoop around his office. I didn't even make it into the building. There was no need." Refilling his glass of wine, he offered his sympathy to Lexy, "If it means anything to you, she wasn't very attractive. I didn't get a good look at her face, but I can promise you, you have a lot more to offer." He looked Lexy up and down.

"Thank you for that. It does help, a little." She ran her tongue over her lips. Setting her glass down, she straightened up her posture. "Do you think there is any truth to the letter? Do you think he is prepping me to kill his wife, and he is already prepping another woman to kill me?" she asked. "It just sounds absurd. I have a hard time believing it." She didn't want to believe it. In her mind, it sounded like a movie script. It was far too preposterous to have any truth to it.

"You know, at this point, nothing is absurd to me. I have heard and seen it all. The air in Charleston is filled with lies and deceit." Rutledge had seen it all. The secrets he had learned, and kept, ranged from boring to downright disturbing. The things people did behind closed doors, hell sometimes right out in public, were astonishing.

It was in Lexy's best interest to believe him. She didn't want to hear another word about it. Without speaking, she straddled Rutledge. He responded quickly and leaned in to kiss her glossy lips. For the next hour, Lexy and Rutledge enjoyed each other. She typically took control with

George, but she enjoyed letting Rutledge take the reins. By the time they were done, George was the furthest thing from Lexy's mind.

"Do you want a glass of water?" Lexy offered Rutledge. She threw an old t-shirt over her head.

"Please," he said as he caught his breath. He put his boxers back on but didn't feel the need to dress any further. Lexy handed him the glass of water and sat down next to him on her couch. "Well-"

"That was fun," Rutledge finished her sentence. He seemed in no hurry to leave, and it was out of the ordinary for Lexy. "I have some groceries at my place. Mind if I go grab them and make us some dinner?"

Lexy's eyes lit up, "Hell no, I don't mind." She certainly wasn't expecting a meal afterward. "Damn, you are setting the bar high."

"It'll take me five minutes," he said while putting the rest of his clothes on. "Be back soon!" She admired his muscular frame while he headed out the door. Lexy took full advantage of the few minutes she had alone and touched up her makeup. The night was unexpected, but she was enjoying her time with Rutledge. It was a nice change of pace from the anxious week she had endured.

Once fifteen minutes had passed and Rutledge

had not returned, Lexy was concerned that he had changed his mind. Although she was confident their business arrangement would ensure his return, her self-doubt still lingered anyway.

Right when Lexy was about to start to feel concerned, Rutledge returned with a large bag full of groceries and a full cooler. "Sorry, I ended up grabbing more than I thought I would," he apologized. "I always buy too many groceries then end up spending most of my meals out to dinner with clients."

Lexy was relieved; she felt stupid for thinking he had stood her up. In addition to the relief she felt, she was grateful that he had food in hand. Her pantry and refrigerator were both empty. An attractive man with groceries in his hands was more than she could ask for. "Oh, please don't apologize! I'm just grateful for food," she smiled at him. "I need to go to the store; I don't have much around here right now."

"Give me an hour, and I'll have dinner ready. It'll be worth the wait," he promised. Lexy's small apartment didn't have a dining room, but she figured the kitchen table would suffice. After she set the table, she watched Rutledge work his magic in the kitchen. She wanted to ask what they were having, but she figured it would be nice to be surprised. After all, she was grateful a man was in her kitchen cooking for her at all. Nora was the only one who had cooked for her there; she was thankful she had let Nora talk her into buying all the necessary tools and equipment.

"I'll serve your bowl and bring it to you," Rutledge suggested. "It might be easier." He stirred whatever was cooking in the large Dutch oven pot. Lexy stood on her tiptoes to try to get a glance at the meal before she took a seat at the table.

"That works for me. What are we having?" she asked as she patiently waited. Rutledge had already found her dinnerware and had two large soup bowls out for them. "Soup?" Lexy guessed when she noticed the bowls.

"We're having shrimp and okra gumbo. Have you ever had it?" Rutledge served their gumbo over beds of rice before carrying the bowls to the table. Lexy shook her head in response. "Let me know if you need anything with it. You won't know until you take a bite."

The gumbo's delicious smell entered Lexy's nostrils as soon as Rutledge placed her bowl in front of her. "This looks fantastic! I don't need anything; it's perfect. Thank you!" She waited for Rutledge to take a seat before she filled her spoon with the gumbo and shoved it into her mouth. "Wow," was the only word Lexy could get out with her mouth full. Once she swallowed, she praised Rutledge, "I wasn't expecting such a nice meal." He waved off her compliments, but deep down, he knew he was pulling out all the stops to impress her.

After dinner, Rutledge was still in no hurry to leave. They cleaned the kitchen together while they chatted; they both wanted to get to know each other better. Their connection was instant and obvious. They had chemistry, and it felt genuine. Lexy felt herself grinning, but she knew she needed to slow her roll. She didn't want to get ahead of herself, and she tended to do that. Though, something about Rutledge seemed different to her. The kind of different she had been searching for all along. She felt hopeful, at the least.

Once Lexy's kitchen was sparkling clean, Rutledge suggested they watch a stand-up comedian he had seen recently and enjoyed. "Are you sure you want to hang out?" Lexy asked him. "Just because we had sex doesn't mean you have to stay, you know."

"What?" Rutledge looked confused. "I want to. I wouldn't be here if I didn't want to be." Rutledge didn't need to convince her any further; Lexy was smitten with him. She shoved her self-doubt into the deepest corner of her mind and allowed herself to accept what he was saying. She was a catch. Why wouldn't he want to spend time with her? They spent most of the evening talking and fell asleep in the wee hours. They avoided any further conversation about George. Neither of them had any interest in discussing him.

The next morning, Lexy woke to a disturbingly bright bedroom. Distracted by Rutledge the evening before, Lexy forgot to draw her curtains. She rolled over to greet Rutledge, but her heart sank when she noticed that he wasn't in the bed with her. There was a note on her bedside table that said, "I'm so sorry I had to leave. I have a meeting at eight, and you looked so peaceful I didn't want to wake you. I'll call you later today." Lexy sighed with relief. She believed him, and that was a different feeling for her. She didn't trust others easily. Nora and her parents were the only people she fully trusted, but she was starting to think she could add Rutledge to the list.

After just one night with Rutledge, she was infatuated. She only got four hours of sleep, but her mind was wide awake. Restless, she got out of bed and started cleaning. If she couldn't sleep, she could at least make use of her energy. She was in the middle of scrubbing her toilet when her phone rang. She tore the yellow rubber gloves off of her hands and ran to answer it, "Hello?"

"Oh, good! You're up," Rutledge's voice greeted her on the other end of the line. "I was worried I would wake you."

Lexy was relieved to hear from him. She patted herself on the back for allowing herself to trust him. "The sun woke me up pretty early. Thanks for leaving a note. I'm not going to lie, I assumed the worst when I woke up and saw you were gone," she admitted. Lexy never shared her insecurities, but for some reason, she felt comfortable admitting it to Rutledge.

"I was worried you would think I bailed. I also considered that you might not see the note, so I called as soon as I could. I had a meeting with a client this morning. I'm planning on taking my boat out this afternoon, but it would be a lot more fun if I had your company. Would you like to go fishing with me?" Rutledge sounded hopeful. Lexy was used to one-night stands, quickies, and married men. No one ever wanted to hang out with her the day after a hookup. She figured he would be sick of her by now.

Lexy looked out her window; it was a beautiful day to be out on the water, and there was no way in hell she was going to pass up more time with Rutledge. "That sounds like fun!" They made plans for Rutledge to pick her up at noon.

Lexy ditched her cleaning for a new task – swimsuit shopping. She rode her bike to Las Olas on King Street to purchase a new bikini. She wanted something that would knock Rutledge's socks off. A lime green Brazilian bikini bottom with a matching bandeau top was her pick. The bandeau offered little support, but that wasn't the purpose of it.

Once she returned home from her retail mission, she had a little over an hour to prepare for her boat day with Rutledge. She showered and put her damp, blonde hair in French braid pigtails. She knew it would be pointless to blow-dry or straighten her hair; she planned on swimming. It was August in Charleston which meant it was mandatory to get in the water to cool off. Though, she did apply her makeup as she normally would. Mentally congratulating herself for investing in a few waterproof versions of her favorite products, she was thankful she didn't have to go barefaced. Her looks were important to her, and she always wanted to appear perfect.

The clock was inching towards noon, and Lexy was almost ready. She loaded a bag with a few necessities including tanning oil, a towel, and water. She considered bringing some liquor, but she wanted to let Rutledge decide whether or not they drank that afternoon. For the first time, she couldn't care less whether or not alcohol was involved. Lexy simply enjoyed Rutledge's company. As long as she was going to be in the sun with him, she was going to have a good day. She was sure of it.

Chapter 11

Rutledge showed up right on time just like the evening before. Lexy felt strongly that his punctuality proved just how seriously he took their new friendship. He stood at her door in board shorts and a t-shirt, and Lexy watched him for a moment through her peephole. He was incredibly attractive. He was much younger than the guys Lexy typically went after.

The moment she opened her door, he embraced her. His tongue explored the depths of her mouth, and they were on the verge of getting lost in the moment. Before it went too far, Lexy pulled away. "Later," she whispered. She straightened her outfit that had wrinkled during their embrace. Her new bikini was on display beneath the sheerness of her cover-up, and she could feel his eyes on her body as she collected her things.

Rutledge opened the passenger door and helped Lexy into his lifted Tahoe. He had fishing rods, coolers, and plenty of gear with him. While Rutledge made his way to the driver seat, Lexy pinched herself to make sure she wasn't dreaming.

How was this attractive and respectful man single? She figured there must be something wrong with him. She was considering the weird or annoying quirks he might have when he broke her train of thought. "I have a boat slip at the Shem Creek Marina," he told her. "The staff is already prepping the boat, so we'll be able to head out when we arrive."

"Sounds good! I didn't bring any drinks. I hope that's okay. I should have asked if you wanted me to," she said as she glanced at the two large coolers propped up behind them. "It looks like you brought more than enough."

He laughed when he realized her assumption. "One of those coolers is empty. I brought it in case we catch some fish!" He explained. "I didn't bring two coolers full of beer. The other one has some sodas, beer, and vodka. I didn't know what you would want, so I brought options." Once they arrived at the Shem Creek Marina, Rutledge loaded his boat with the coolers and gear, and they headed off.

As they cruised by the waterfront restaurants on Shem Creek, they noticed how packed they all were. "It's nice to be alone. Don't get me wrong, I love going out! It's nice to enjoy some peace though." Lexy removed her cover-up as they went by Red's Ice House. A guy whistled at her from the bar, and Rutledge gave him the finger. "Nice," Lexy said in response to Rutledge's gesture.

"A pretty little thing like you deserves more respect than some asshole catcalling you from across the water," he said in defense of his actions. Lexy liked that he stood up for her. It didn't seem like he had done it out of jealousy. Rather, he truly thought she deserved respect. It was flattering, and she appreciated it. She had encountered far more catcallers than defenders in her day.

Rutledge had a center console boat, and Lexy made herself at home on the bow while he steered them into the Charleston Harbor. His eyes were on her, but his sunglasses made his constant staring discreet. Her skimpy bikini left little to the imagination, and he already knew what was hiding underneath it. He couldn't stop thinking about the night before. He started to get aroused and had to distract himself. "Where would you like to go?" Rutledge asked Lexy while he thought about anything other than her revealing swimsuit.

She shrugged her shoulders and reached into the cooler for a beer, "Anywhere!" She cracked the can open, taking a few gulps. Her lime green bikini popped against the bright blue background of the ocean and sky. Rutledge navigated the boat to a familiar fishing spot. They chatted about their interests and experiences while they cast their lines. Lexy was the first to have a tug on hers, and she wasn't sure what to do.

"Help me!" Lexy panicked for a moment but was able to reel in a flounder with minimal help from Rutledge. Although she had been out in boats with guys who were fishing many times, she had never actually participated. She had underestimated her abilities; it wasn't that hard to reel it in.

"Damn! Great job, Lexy!" Rutledge congratulated her, but the look of surprise on his face told her that he hadn't expected her to catch anything that day. "Hate to break it to you, but we're going to have to let this one go," he removed the hook from the corner of the fish's mouth. "It doesn't meet the size requirements to keep it."

"Wait! Take a picture of me holding it!" She handed her phone to Rutledge and posed with the fish, holding it as far away from her body as she could. Once she got her shot for Instagram, Rutledge tossed it back into the water. Lexy looked disappointed, and Rutledge tried to cheer her up, "It's a good sign! I think you'll land a big one today." She smiled at his encouraging words.

"I think I might go for a swim before we recast our lines," she took off her cover-up and slowly climbed down the boat's ladder. As she swam around, she hoped Rutledge wouldn't figure out the real reason why she got into the water. She needed to pee.

"I'll join you!" He shouted before jumping into the water. Thankfully, she had already finished relieving herself. They swam around for a few minutes. "It's nice to cool off." The water was warm, but it still offered refreshing relief from the hot sun.

They made their way back onto the boat, and Lexy opened another beer. "At this rate, you'll have to carry me off the boat later," Lexy joked. "Especially drinking like this on an empty stomach," she added. "I should have had lunch."

Rutledge opened the cooler that was designated for their potential future catches. "I brought along some sandwiches for us if you want one," he offered. He handed her a homemade turkey sandwich on sourdough bread. It had lettuce, tomato, and all the fixings. "One has mustard and one has mayonnaise. I didn't know what you would prefer, and I guess it was risky to assume that you even liked one of the two."

"Shut. Up." Lexy said in response causing a confused look to creep onto Rutledge's face. "Did you seriously make us sandwiches?"

Rutledge looked self-conscious about his decision. "Is that a bad thing?" he asked.

Lexy pressed her body against his and kissed him in response to his question. "It's perfect," Lexy said. "I can be a real bitch when I'm hangry. I wouldn't want you to see that side of me this early on. Which do you prefer, mustard or mayonnaise?"

"I'm more of a mayonnaise guy, but I like them both. Otherwise, it would have been dangerous to make one of each," he awkwardly laughed.

She picked up the sandwich that had mustard. "Funny, I prefer mustard," she said as she took a bite. "Works out perfectly." She moaned in exaggeration while chewing. "It is so good. Thank you!"

"For the record, I can't imagine you being a bitch, but I'll try to remember to keep you well-fed to avoid meeting that side of you," he promised with a sly smile. She nudged him, fully aware that he was making fun of her.

After they finished their sandwiches, their concentration immediately went back to fishing. Rutledge caught a sixteen-inch flounder, and at that length, it met the size requirements to take it home with them. He stored it on the ice in the empty cooler. Lexy never had another tug on her line, but she was proud of herself for catching a fish at all. She stepped out of her comfort zone, and that in itself was an accomplishment for her. They eventually made their way back to the Shem Creek Marina. After Rutledge transferred his gear from the boat to his Tahoe, he dropped the boat off with the staff of the marina.

Besides the photo Rutledge had snapped for

her, Lexy barely checked her phone all afternoon. She had been so preoccupied with her new friend, she hadn't felt the need to. It was refreshing to feel disconnected from the world. When she finally went through her unread text messages, she was surprised to see they were all from George. He had invited himself over, once again, that evening. Lexy rolled her eyes and placed her phone back in her bag. She didn't even take the time to listen to the voicemail he had left her; he wasn't worth it.

"I should make us fish tacos with this flounder tonight," Rutledge suggested while he drove them back to their apartments downtown. "I can whip up some in no time. You'll love them." Lexy's jaw dropped, and she quickly closed her mouth before Rutledge noticed. She couldn't believe that, yet again, he was proposing that they spend more time together. She needed to stop acting so shocked; maybe that was the kind of treatment she was supposed to be getting from men.

"Would you mind if I freshened up first?" She asked excitedly. After their long day on the boat, her skin was sticky with salt water, and her fine hair was windblown and tangled.

"Not at all. Text me when you're ready. Since I live only a few blocks away, I'll walk over to meet you. We can walk over to my place together," he suggested as they pulled in front of her apartment. "Is that okay with you? I can drive over if you prefer."

Lexy had planned on wearing heels, but she loved the idea of Rutledge walking over to escort her. To her, it seemed old school and romantic. She could easily change her outfit. "I would love to walk over together! I'll text you." She hopped out of his vehicle and disappeared into her apartment. Rutledge patted himself on the back; the two of them were getting along really well.

Chapter 12

While Lexy was in the shower, she heard a knock at her front door. Her first instinct was that it was Rutledge; she assumed he had forgotten something. She didn't have her phone in the bathroom with her, so she didn't know if he had tried to call.

Nine times out of ten, Lexy faithfully used her peephole. She wasn't thinking straight that evening, unfortunately, and she opened her door without looking out first. She expected to see Rutledge and was shocked to see George standing in her doorway instead. He tried to enter, but Lexy successfully blocked him. Luckily, her neighbor was arriving home at the same time, and it was a perfect excuse to usher George out.

"I can't talk right now. I have plans. I will call you," Lexy said in a raised voice to draw the attention of her neighbor. Her neighbor, now on high alert, waited in the hall until George left the building. Lexy gave her a nod of appreciation before she returned to the safety of her apartment. She double bolted her door before she realized how much her hands were shaking. She grabbed her phone and called Rutledge, the one person she could trust.

"Hey! Are you ready?" he asked. "That was quick! I can be over in a jiffy."

"No, no. I'm not. George…" was all Lexy could get out. She took a deep breath and regained control of her speech. "George just came by here. I'm really freaked out." She didn't want George to ruin her evening with Rutledge, but she was distraught. If the letter was true, she felt as if she should be fearful for her life.

"Do you want me to come over there?" Rutledge offered. "I can hang out while you finish getting ready." He sounded sincere, and she appreciated his concern.

Lexy's heart had finally calmed to its normal beat. She was grateful that Rutledge cared for her; she needed someone she could turn to. "No, thank you though. I'm okay. I'm going to finish getting ready, and then I'll text you. I'm sorry about all of this. Let's just try to forget it." She was determined to enjoy her evening.

With conditioner still in her hair, Lexy returned to the shower to rinse it out. While she blow-dried her hair, she turned off the appliance every few minutes to listen for any noise near her front door. No matter how hard she tried to push the negative thoughts out of her head, she couldn't. She felt paranoid; the sooner she could be out of her apartment, the better.

She straightened her hair and applied her makeup in record time, moving as quickly as she could while still ensuring she looked her best. A strapless gold top with white denim shorts was her outfit choice, and she paired it with comfortable wedges that she knew she wouldn't have any trouble walking in. Although she had planned on wearing sandals, she preferred the way an elevated heel made her legs look. It wasn't a far walk anyway; she could handle it.

When she was close to being ready, she went ahead and let Rutledge know. She knew his presence would calm her; she couldn't wait another minute. She regretted not letting him come over when he first offered, but she wasn't used to relying on others. She hated asking for help.

In no time, Rutledge appeared at her front door. She double-checked the peephole before opening it. Even though she was confident it was Rutledge, she couldn't be too sure. When she opened the door earlier, George's face was the last thing she expected to see. It was something she wouldn't soon forget. He had crossed a line. It scared the hell out of her, and she would never let it happen again.

"Why don't you spend the night at my place

tonight? I don't want you to have to deal with George trying to come back for another visit later," Rutledge looked worried.

Lexy appreciated his offer; she was already dreading returning to her apartment later. She knew she would enjoy the evening more if it wasn't in the back of her mind. "If you're sure you're okay with it," she said. They had spent nearly the entire weekend together, and she didn't want to overstep his boundaries.

"Pack something to sleep in, or don't," he winked, "and whatever else you need for the night before we head over to my place." He took a seat on her couch, making it clear he wasn't in a hurry. She quickly packed a couple of things, and they were on their way.

It was early in the evening, but the temperature hadn't dropped in the slightest. It was a hot, calm day. Lexy was worried she would break a sweat; she would give anything for a breeze to come by. She tried her best to focus on her surroundings. The houses were full of character, and she enjoyed admiring them. No matter how many times she walked around downtown, she found something new to appreciate about the charming city. When Rutledge reached for her hand, she had to deny him. "I'm sorry; I don't want my hand to get all sweaty against yours. You'll think I'm gross," she explained.

"I would never think you are gross, but if it's unbearable for you, we don't need to hold hands," he said. He was trying to be understanding. A light breeze blew by them, immediately cooling her down. She was thankful for it. "We're almost to my apartment, anyway."

When Lexy walked into Rutledge's apartment, she immediately took a step back. Her eyes shone with amazement. His bachelor pad was unlike anything she expected; it was beautifully decorated. Lexy glanced around at the unique artwork that hung on his walls. She had assumed a Budweiser poster would be the art he featured, but she was wrong. She considered that maybe an ex-girlfriend was responsible for the décor. "Did you pick all of this out?" Lexy pointed around the room.

"Yes. Everyone assumes an ex-girlfriend did it for me, because how could a man like me have such exquisite taste? Right?" Lexy blushed knowing he had read her mind. Rutledge laughed, "My mom is an interior designer. I grew up around it, and I developed a particular taste. That's all."

While Lexy looked around the room, she noticed there weren't any personal photographs. The artwork that was on display was stunning, but it felt impersonal. There was no homey vibe to his apartment; it was rather cold.

Rutledge headed into the immaculate kitchen, and Lexy followed closely behind him. "Are you hungry?" Lexy asked. She hoped his answer would be yes; she was famished.

"Starving!" He responded eagerly. "I already filleted the flounder so that you wouldn't have to witness that part." He pulled the fish out of the refrigerator and added oil to a pan on the stovetop, turning the heat up. He cut the filets of flounder into smaller, more manageable pieces, and tossed them in a milk bath. One by one, he dredged the pieces in flour before tossing them into the hot oil. He repeated this process until all of the pieces of fish had been fried.

Meanwhile, Lexy worked on preparing the toppings. Rutledge had an array of fresh ingredients in his refrigerator. From red onions to cilantro, the options were endless. They loaded their fish tacos and carried their plates to Rutledge's dining room table. Once they had both sat down, Lexy took her first bite. "This is delicious! This is the fish you caught today?"

Rutledge enjoyed the praise, but responded casually, "Yeah, no big deal. I do this all the time! Stick around, and you'll find that out."

"It's the best fish taco I've ever had," Lexy acclaimed.

"I can't take all the credit," he reminded her. "There's nothing like eating fish the same day you caught it. It's as fresh as it comes!" He made a fair point.

They both finished everything on their plates, and Lexy even considered going back for more. She decided that she didn't want to feel bloated while spending the night with Rutledge so she went without the second helping.

They cleared their dishes together, but Rutledge refused to let Lexy clean when she offered. "It can be done later," he insisted. "Come sit with me." He took a seat on the larger of the two leather sofas in his living room. Gesturing for her to sit next to him, he asked Alexa to dim the lights in the room.

Lexy wasn't really in the mood for anything quite yet. Her stomach was still full from the tacos. "Do you mind if we hang out for a bit?" She asked. "I'm stuffed."

He realized she thought he was coming on to her and swiftly apologized, "I'm sorry. I didn't mean for it to seem like that's where this was going. I'm just tired from our day in the sun, and tired from that meal, so I wanted to sit with you for a little while and talk."

Feeling guilty that she had assumed he meant something else, Lexy lowered her guard and sat down next to him. He reached for her right foot and pulled it into his lap, massaging her heel. "I haven't had a foot massage in so long," Lexy rested her head on the throw pillow behind her. At some point, she dozed off.

She woke a couple of hours later in Rutledge's dark living room. A soft blanket was covering her, and she could see a hint of light coming from a doorway down the short hall. She had never even made it to his bedroom. He was a true gentleman. She tiptoed over to the door that had light seeping out from under it and knocked softly, "Rutledge?"

He opened the door and embraced her, "I was hoping you would wake up at some point! I drifted off to sleep on the couch too, but I woke up about an hour ago. I came in here to go through some emails. I didn't want any light to disturb you; I hope I didn't wake you!" He was so kind to her. The more respect he showed her, the harder she fell for him. In the past, she had never been interested in nice guys. Stupidly, she thought that kindness showed weakness. She was starting to realize that she had it all wrong; nice guys were the strongest.

Lexy was no longer feeling full. Instead, she was feeling frisky. Her nap had replenished her energy. She pulled Rutledge onto his bed and had her way with him.

Chapter 13

"Do you want something to snack on?" Rutledge offered Lexy. It was a little after eleven o'clock, and both of them were wide awake. "I could go for a beer," he opened his refrigerator and selected a stout.

"A beer sounds good to me!" Lexy studied his selection and picked a pale ale. "I'm not going to lie, I'm contemplating pulling out the leftover flounder and making myself another taco," she admitted. She had worked up an appetite.

Rutledge pulled the leftovers out and handed them to her, "Go for it! Don't be shy." She accepted the leftovers and reheated enough to fill a taco. She ate it in a few bites and was thankful she had given in to her urge. They carried their beers over to his couch and placed them on coasters. "Would you like to watch a movie or talk?" Rutledge asked. "I wouldn't mind getting to know each other a little better."

"I would love to chat. We can watch a movie another time." She crossed her legs and reached for her beer. Lexy enjoyed her conversations with Rutledge. They weren't filled with awkward silences like her conversations with George, and he didn't make her feel stupid like George did. "Tell me more about yourself," she requested. Rutledge told her just about everything she could possibly want to know. From his childhood in the Lowcountry to his college days, Lexy heard it all. Every new piece of information was like another piece to the Rutledge puzzle. His strong moral character made more sense once she heard more about his upbringing.

Rutledge was equally as interested in hearing about Lexy. He asked her plenty of questions and inquired about her which was something George never did. The difference between Rutledge and George was astonishing; Lexy wasn't quite sure what she saw in George.

At some point, they got on the subject of her former lover. "Do you think George's second wife killed his first wife?" Lexy asked Rutledge. They were on their third beers by that point and were joking around. Lexy's question was anything but a joke though. She was curious to hear Rutledge's opinion.

"It's possible," Rutledge confirmed. "As I've said before, anything is possible. I've seen and heard things you would never be able to guess. Honestly, I find it suspicious that both of his wives died from accidents. If he didn't convince someone to do it, then he probably staged the accidents himself." Lexy nodded. He was right; George was probably capable of murder.

"Well, I have to do something. Do you think the police would believe me?" Lexy asked, but the answer to her question was obvious. If she took the letter to the police, they would think she was crazy and dismiss her accusations as quickly as she made them.

"No way," Rutledge confirmed what she already knew. "You have no evidence to show them, besides the letter, and that isn't much. Anyone can fabricate a letter. You can't use the evidence I illegally obtained for you. Plus, let's be real. He has money, and money is powerful. He would lawyer up and come out just fine. He could even turn around and sue you for damages."

Lexy considered her options for a moment. It didn't seem like she had any. "So, I'll just live afraid, aware that he could either have me killed or kill me himself at any time," she said dramatically. Maybe it was the alcohol going to her head, but she wanted a better solution. "He needs to be stopped."

Rutledge looked intrigued. "How do you suggest we stop him?" he asked. She didn't respond, but he could tell she was plotting. "You could give him the fate he planned for you," he suggested. It was a dark, devious suggestion. Rutledge wasn't sure how Lexy would respond to the idea.

"You mean, I should kill him? Before he gets the chance to kill me?" The curious look on Lexy's face concerned Rutledge; it was obvious she was already considering it. "I guess we would be saving his current wife as well. I mean, he'll just find someone to replace me if we don't stop him." Lexy's thin eyebrows raised, "Are you sure we're right?" Lexy thought back to earlier that evening when George unexpectedly showed up at her door. There was a look in his eyes that told her the letter was true.

The bright light from the refrigerator flooded the room when Rutledge went to retrieve another beer. "Want one?"

"Sure, why the hell not." Lexy stretched out her legs into the spot where Rutledge had been sitting.

Rutledge clinked the bottles together as he pulled them out of the refrigerator. When he returned to his seat, he gently set Lexy's smooth, tanned legs in his lap. Caressing her soft skin, he finally answered her question, "I've always trusted evidence. Evidence doesn't lie – never has. There is plenty of it to show you who George really is. It's your choice whether or not you want to believe it." They were both pretty tipsy, and neither of them needed the additional beer. With their beers more than halfway full, they left them on the coffee table and made their way to Rutledge's bedroom. While they were kissing they both drifted off to sleep, tangled in each other's arms.

The next morning, Lexy woke up before Rutledge. She rushed to the bathroom to touch-up her makeup and brush her teeth. She wanted him to wake up to a perfect version of her. Returning to bed, she gasped when she noticed the white pillow on Rutledge's bed was painted with her makeup. She was mortified. She took the pillowcase off and ran into the hall to locate his washing machine.

Running around his apartment, she was having a hard time finding his laundry room. "Can I help you?" Rutledge stood in the door of his bedroom in his boxers.

Lexy turned a blazing shade of red. Caught in her tracks, she waved the pillowcase as if were to signal her surrender. "I ruined your pillowcase. I'm so sorry; I'll take it home with me and wash it. If I can't get the stains out, I'll buy you a new one." She looked like a child who had been caught using her mother's lipstick to draw on the walls.

Rutledge took the pillowcase out of her hand and tossed it into the corner of the room. "I don't care about a damn pillowcase. As long as you're comfortable, you can ruin all of my pillows. Come back to bed with me," he grabbed her hand. She willingly did as she was told.

The two of them were extremely compatible in the bedroom. From the first time they met, Lexy felt a sense of comfort when she was around Rutledge. It made their lovemaking better than she thought was possible. Their deeper connection changed everything, and for the first time, Lexy understood emotional intimacy. All of Lexy's past relationships were based on lust, lies, and manipulation. None of it had ever been real, raw emotion like she felt with Rutledge. It scared the shit out of her, but she was finally ready to admit to herself that she was already falling in love with Rutledge.

"I can make you some breakfast if you would like. Whatever you want - pancakes, waffles, bacon, eggs. You name it, and I'll make it," he proposed. Rutledge was always so willing to please. In the past, this trait in other men would come off as needy and pathetic to Lexy, but Rutledge's actions made her feel differently. It made her feel cared for and wanted.

They had spent nearly the entire weekend together. Lexy felt strongly that a little space would make them eager to see each other. "You're sweet to offer, but I have to decline. I need to head home and get some chores done before Monday sneaks up on me," she explained.

"I'll drive you. You don't need to walk home in

your pajamas or last night's outfit," he grabbed his keys, and they climbed into his Tahoe. It was only a couple of minutes before they arrived at Lexy's apartment. "When can I see you again?" He asked as she jumped out of his large vehicle.

Her bleached teeth glimmered in the sun when she smiled back at him, "Soon. You have my number." She blew him a kiss before doing a runway walk for him, swaying her hips dramatically, to her apartment door. He waited for her to enter her residence before pulling out of his parking spot. Instinctively, he looked around to make sure no one had been watching her apartment. He didn't know exactly what George was capable of, but he was going to make sure nothing happened to Lexy.

Chapter 14

The condition of Lexy's apartment proved she had been busy over the weekend. The sets of scrubs she had worn to work the week before were still jammed into her laundry basket, begging to be washed. There was a sink full of dishes that needed to be done, and her beauty products were scattered all over her bathroom counter. She threw her hair into a ponytail and got to work.

The evening before, she thought she would never feel comfortable alone inside her apartment again. George's spontaneous visit had shaken her up, and she didn't think she would recover so quickly. After her evening with Rutledge, she felt relaxed. There was something about him that she found comforting; she was confident that he wouldn't let anything happen to her.

Little by little, she conquered her chores. Finishing around five, she had plenty of time for her favorite Sunday evening routine - a bubble bath, a glass of wine, and Bravo. While Lexy soaked in her bath, she considered how different life would be for her if she had a boyfriend. She wouldn't be able to have her bubble bath and wine nights followed by a Bravo binge – or would she? Maybe Rutledge wouldn't care how she liked to spend her time.

With wet hair and a refilled wine glass, Lexy folded her last load of laundry while The Real Housewives of Beverly Hills played on her television. "This is the life," she said to herself before chuckling in embarrassment. Maybe single life wasn't all it was cracked up to be. Maybe she did want someone to come home to and to cook dinner with. She wanted someone to say goodnight to, in the same bed as her, every night. As much as she had pushed the idea away in the past, there was no stopping it now. Rutledge had permanently changed the wiring in Lexy's brain. She wanted the fairy tale, and she wanted it with Rutledge.

Lexy rejoiced when she found leftover gumbo from Friday night in her refrigerator. She never saw Rutledge store the leftovers, but it was sweet of him to do so. She sent him a quick text to thank him for his thoughtful act while the gumbo reheated on the stovetop. They texted back and forth for a couple of hours and eventually made plans for the following evening. Filled with happiness, Lexy fell asleep early in the comfort of her own bed.

The following morning, Lexy was in a cheerful mood at work. She spent extra time chatting with each patient, offered to help her fellow nurses, and even picked up lunch for the office. Her coworkers took notice of her positive energy and seemed pleased with the new and approved version of Lexy. She had always been a hard worker, but she had never been exceptionally pleasant to be around. As she went about her day, her mind kept wandering back to Rutledge. He was quite a catch, and she was ecstatic that he had entered her life.

She enjoyed daydreaming about Rutledge, but the thought of him almost always led her back to the letter. She didn't want to underestimate George, and she knew she would hear from him again soon. Determined to be prepared for his next contact with her, she tried to come up with a solution. She had considered playing nice with George. She could attempt to end things cordially; she could simply tell him that she had met someone else. Though, that wouldn't be a strong enough excuse for a man who easily has affairs while posing as happily married. Judging from his past, he didn't believe in monogamy.

Although her day was moving along smoothly, Lexy wished the clock would move faster. She wasn't used to having evening plans to look forward to during the weekdays. Most of the men she had been involved with in the past had spent their weeks with their wives and families. It had been years since she had any romantic plans during the week that didn't involve sex and a quick departure.

That evening, Rutledge brought take-out over to her apartment. Lexy enjoyed having someone to talk to after work, and she told Rutledge a few funny stories from her day. He shared as well, though the events of his day had to be kept a little more private. He had met with a client, and without sharing names or too many details, Rutledge told Lexy the gist of it.

They enjoyed each other's company, and she invited him to stay the night. The two of them disappeared behind her bedroom door early in the evening. At some point during the middle of the night, Rutledge's phone rang. He left shortly after with no explanation, but Lexy was too groggy to mind. With her eyes half shut, she stumbled across her apartment to deadbolt her door. As soon as she got back in bed, she was fast asleep.

When she woke Tuesday morning, she was still unbothered by Rutledge's sudden departure in the middle of the night. In less than a week, he had gained her trust. She knew there must have been a good reason as to why he left, and she felt confident she would hear from him soon.

By lunchtime, Lexy had still not heard from Rutledge. While she was eating a salad she had picked up from Publix, she received a text message from Nora. When the message first came in, she was hoping it would be from Rutledge, but it was good to hear from Nora. She hadn't talked to her in a few days. Lexy responded to her attentive best friend and returned to her salad.

The rest of her day went by without any contact from Rutledge. Lexy tried to not let it bother her, but she couldn't help it. She considered that he could be in some kind of danger. His line of business was risky, and she felt it was only logical to be concerned about him. Finally, just after nine o'clock that night, he called her. "I'm sorry I disappeared last night. I had no intention of leaving, but something came up. I haven't had a free second to call you until now." He assumed she was angry and pleaded with her.

"I'm just happy to hear your voice." She didn't feel the need to ask any questions. She assumed his disappearance was work-related, and she knew that he couldn't talk about his clients. They chatted for a while, and Rutledge started to doze off. Eventually, they said goodnight and hung up their phones.

On Wednesday, they kept a similar routine. Rutledge had again spent his day with clients and in meetings. A phone conversation was all he had the energy for. Lexy didn't mind one bit. She thought their conversations over the phone felt just as intimate as their time spent together.

The only negative side of their time apart was

the free time Lexy had to focus on the insane predicament she was in. At work, she found her mind filled with thoughts and questions about the mysterious letter she had received.

While Lexy was getting ready for work Thursday morning, the text notification sound dinged on her phone. Assuming the early morning message was from Rutledge, she excitedly retrieved her phone from her bedside table. Her phone's lock screen displayed the message's preview, and Lexy's entire body tensed when she saw who the sender was. It was the last person she wanted to hear from - George. The message read, "You've had an early bedtime this week." Lexy drew a sharp breath as she read the first line. Had he been watching her? She kept reading the lengthy message, "I want to see you. I don't know what I did to upset you, but please let me make it up to you. I miss you." was all it said. With trembling hands, she took a screenshot of the message from George and sent it directly to Rutledge.

A couple of minutes later, her phone was ringing. "Hey," she greeted Rutledge on the other end of the line.

"Did you respond?" He asked her.

"No, of course not. I don't know what to say. At some point, I think I want to say something. Or do something. I don't know. I have to figure it out." She felt panicked and couldn't articulate what she was feeling. They both needed to start their days, and they got off the phone.

While she finished getting ready, Lexy considered all the ways she could approach her situation with George. She wanted more than anything to contact the police and let them handle it. At least, she wanted a restraining order from George. The text message should be enough proof that he had been watching her. Lexy was terrified; she didn't know what George was capable of. She was distracted for the remainder of the day. The overproductive Lexy her coworkers experienced on Monday was already long gone.

When Lexy reached out to Rutledge to make plans that evening, she was disappointed to learn that he was once again busy. She spent the evening alone with her thoughts and a bottle of wine. The more she thought about the scenario she was dealing with, the more she realized that something drastic needed to happen. Even Rutledge had suggested that she take care of George once and for all. Maybe it was the wine talking, but she knew one thing was true: if one of them was going to die, it had to be George.

Chapter 15

By the time Friday morning rolled around, Lexy was itching to do something away from her apartment. She had been constantly afraid that George would show up at her door again, and she couldn't spend another night alone with her thoughts there. Not wanting to come off as needy to Rutledge, she reached out to Nora. She missed her best friend, and they made plans to have a girls' night that evening.

Typically, their girls' nights involved bars, boys, and too much booze. Their plans were a little different for that evening; they were going to have dinner at Nora's condo. Lexy loved it when she cooked for her. With plans to head over to Nora's directly after work, Lexy took some clothes with her to change into. She didn't want to eat dinner in her scrubs.

The workday passed by slowly for Lexy. Although she was looking forward to her plans that evening, she found herself wishing she would hear from Rutledge. Even a short text message would do. She continuously checked her phone, but it only taunted her with no new notifications.

The sun was still high in the sky when Lexy made her way to the Isle of Palms Connector that evening. Salt marshes surrounded her, and she rolled down her window to catch a whiff of their familiar smell. Nearing the top of the connector, Lexy could see the Atlantic Ocean in front of her. No matter how many times she admired the beauty around her, she never stopped feeling lucky to live in such a magical place.

Suddenly, her phone started to ring. She wrestled with her bag, trying to keep her eyes on the road and retrieve her phone at the same time. She answered it as soon as she saw it was Rutledge calling. Only a few minutes away from Nora's condo, Lexy knew she didn't have much time to chat.

Although he seemed disappointed to learn that she already made plans with her friend, he tried to be supportive. "I'm glad you're spending time with your best friend," he said. "I was just hoping to see you. After the week I've had, I could use your company."

A part of Lexy regretted making plans with Nora. She had been anxious to see Rutledge all week, and there was nothing she wanted more than to go be with him. At the same time, she knew her evening with Nora would be good for her. There was always time to see Rutledge later. "Will you come over when I get home in a couple of hours?" She asked Rutledge.

He didn't even hesitate, "Of course."

"I won't be very late," she promised him just before parking at Nora's. "I'll call you when I'm headed home."

As soon as Lexy entered her friend's home, her stomach started to growl. The delicious smell coming from Nora's kitchen had taken over the entire condo. Truthfully, her neighbors were probably drooling as well. "What is that smell?" Lexy asked as she hugged Nora's waist.

With a spoon in one hand, Nora gave Lexy a half-hug. "Take a guess. It's one of your favorites."

Lexy closed her eyes. "It's seafood," she said with certainty. "I knew that in the hall." She took in the smell around her, "If you're making me shrimp and grits, then you get the best friend of the year award."

Nora took the lid off the pot in front of her to show Lexy the grits. "I get that award every year! My dad and his buddy went shrimping the other day. I told him we were having dinner tonight, and he insisted I take some off his hands. He didn't have to ask twice."

Lexy considered telling Nora about the shrimp gumbo and fish tacos Rutledge made for her the past weekend, but she hadn't even told

Nora about Rutledge at all yet. She wanted to ease into it. She opened Nora's refrigerator to get an inventory of her beverage selection. "What are we drinking tonight?"

"Whatever you want. I have some rum and vodka in the freezer." When Nora offered her liquor, Lexy realized that Nora had assumed she would be staying the night.

Lexy retrieved a beer and closed the refrigerator. "If it's cool with you, I'm going to have a beer. I have to head out after dinner, so I don't want to drink too much."

Nora's face fell. She had missed her best friend, and she felt disconnected from her. "What have you been up to lately?" She tried not to show her annoyance, but she was too easy to read.

"Come on, don't be mad at me," Lexy pleaded with her. "I'm so excited to have dinner with you! I can't believe you made shrimp and grits!" She didn't purposefully ignore Nora's question, but it was more convenient to focus on their dinner.

Nora ran over to the stovetop when Lexy mentioned the food. "It's ready!" They loaded their bowls with the traditional Lowcountry meal before heading to Nora's oceanfront porch to eat. They chatted while they ate, and Lexy made a point to compliment the meal multiple times. "This might be the best serving of shrimp and grits I've ever had," she claimed. Nora rolled her eyes, but Lexy wasn't exaggerating. Her friend had skills in the kitchen.

After dinner, Lexy popped open a second beer while the sky started to turn a light shade of pink. They didn't have a direct view of the sunset from Nora's porch; her Isle of Palms view was better for sunrises. Though, they still got to witness the display of color the sunset created. While they admired the sky, Nora rephrased her earlier question. "Did you meet someone? Besides George?"

"Yes," Lexy admitted. Nora waited for her to elaborate further, but Lexy remained quiet.

Nora nudged her with her elbow. "Come on! What's with you?"

Lexy covered her face with her hands. "I'm sorry. Part of me doesn't want to talk about it because I'm afraid I'll jinx it." Rutledge was the first man to show interest in Lexy that didn't have a wife, kids, or a laundry list of affairs.

"Don't be silly. You're not going to jinx it. If you're not ready to talk about it, I won't push you to. Can I ask one more question though?" Lexy nodded, and Nora wasted no time before continuing, "Are you done with George?"

Lexy mentally flashed back to the mysterious letter, George's surprise visit, and his recent text message. For a moment, she considered telling Nora everything she had learned about George from Rutledge. She desperately wanted to confide in her best friend. She wanted to tell her how afraid she was, and she wanted to have someone else on her side. Instead, "Yes," was all that squeaked out of the wimpish woman.

Nora believed her, but she could tell there was more to the story. She knew Lexy never responded well to being pushed for information, so she let it go. Nora told Lexy about Wyatt's plans to come down to visit soon. Nora and Wyatt had talked on the phone every night since he returned home to Charlotte, and they were building a solid foundation for a relationship. Lexy was surprised to hear that they were even still talking. She should have reached out to Nora before to see how everything was going. Lately, Lexy had been a bad friend. She had only been concerned with her own life.

The two women wrapped up their evening and promised to get together again soon. Before Lexy headed out, Nora embraced her. "I'm here. I'll always be here. When you're ready to talk, I'm ready to listen." Nora reminded Lexy what she already knew.

Chapter 16

Once Nora's condo was out of sight, Lexy waited a few minutes before she called Rutledge. "I'm headed home," she informed him. "Will you meet me there? It should only take me twenty minutes or so." She had made every green light on her drive so far, and she was feeling optimistic.

"I'll be there, waiting for you," he promised. "I'll also make sure there are no creeps around." Lexy felt a sense of relief. She wouldn't be going home to an empty apartment or the fear of George waiting at her door. She was going home to Rutledge.

"Remind me, I should get you a key," she casually mentioned. "You shouldn't have to wait outside my door for me." Lexy realized after she said it that the statement was too much. They hadn't even known each other for two weeks, and she was offering him a key to her apartment. She was moving too fast, and she was going to freak him out.

"That would come in handy!" Rutledge's enthusiastic response to Lexy's suggestion made her smile. "Drive safely. I'll see you soon." They both hung up the phone, and Lexy could feel herself buzzing with joy. Rutledge made her feel more wanted than any man ever had, and she wanted him right back. She turned up her radio, and 'Good As Hell' had just come on. She belted it out as if she was Lizzo herself.

When she turned onto her street, Lexy silenced the pop music that had just been blaring through her speakers. She saw Rutledge's Tahoe as she approached her apartment, and the warm and fuzzy feeling returned to her stomach once again. He appeared at her car's door as soon as her ignition turned off. "I was wondering how long you were going to make me wait," he lowered his mouth to Lexy's and gently kissed her on the lips before opening the car door to help her out. As soon as she was standing, she pressed her body against his and kissed him with force.

"Get a room," a kid on a bicycle shouted at them. Rutledge threw his middle finger into the air and continued to kiss Lexy, groping her backside.

"Come on," Lexy giggled, pulling Rutledge towards her apartment door. "We can continue this inside." As soon as her apartment door shut, Lexy and Rutledge's hands were exploring each other's bodies. They were too lost in the moment to notice Lexy's living room blinds were wide open.

"I hope no one saw that," Lexy pulled the throw blanket off of her couch and wrapped it around her naked body. "Probably should have closed these before we did that," she laughed as she closed the blinds and curtains. "That's better."

Rutledge was still naked when she turned around, and Lexy admired his body. She loved that he wasn't quick to dress afterward. Lexy dropped her blanket and joined Rutledge in the nude on the couch. "I could get used to this," Rutledge joked. Though, Lexy hoped he was serious. She could get used to it as well.

Eventually, the two dressed and made their way to the kitchen. "Do you want popcorn with our movie? Dessert? What are you in the mood for?" Lexy asked, but she knew there wasn't much to offer at her apartment. She kept the bare minimum around along with a few snack items.

"I could have a second helping of you," he winked at her. Lexy motioned that she was vomiting, and they both broke out into laughter. The more time they spent together, the more comfortable they felt around each other. "Let's have some popcorn for now."

The bag of popcorn audibly popped in the microwave while they looked through Netflix's endless selection of movies. "I feel like I spend more time looking for a movie than I spend watching the movie," Lexy admitted. "In this case, I hope I spend more time kissing the cute guy on my couch than selecting or watching a movie." Rutledge moved towards her after hearing her comment, but she shooed him away. "We still have to pick a movie first!"

"You choose! I'm happy with anything," Rutledge said on his way to silence the microwave's beeping. Lexy was flattered that he cared more about being with her than the activities they did together. He was easy to please, and she enjoyed lounging around with him. Rutledge was still standing in the kitchen when Lexy's phone received a text message. Assuming she would want to read the message, Rutledge carried her phone in one hand while balancing the large bowl of popcorn in the other. "Here you go," he handed her the phone without taking a peek at the lit-up screen.

The message preview on her locked screen already told Lexy what she didn't want to know. George was the sender of the message. Lexy threw her phone down and ran around her apartment to make sure every set of blinds and curtains were closed. Suddenly, she felt as though they were being watched. "What's going on?" Rutledge asked her, but he had a gut feeling. "The message was from George, wasn't it? What did he say?"

Lexy realized that she never actually read the message and dug her phone out of the crack of her couch cushions it had slipped into. The text from George read, "I miss you. I now know with certainty that you're the woman for me. Please accompany me on my boat next weekend. We can leave on Friday and take a trip to Hilton Head Island. An entire weekend, just the two of us, what do you say?" She read the message over and over again. For a moment, she considered that maybe he did miss her. He had been stuck with Penelope for the last couple of weeks, and he was probably remembering just how boring life was with her.

"What's going on?" Rutledge was still waiting for a response from Lexy. Although Lexy considered it for a moment, she knew she couldn't trust George. Part of her did miss him, but she knew who the monster was hiding behind the man. He was a murderer, even if indirectly, and his previous wives' deaths were on his hands. She knew he would try to manipulate her again at some point, but she wasn't falling for it. "George asked me to go away with him next weekend. That's what the message says. He wants me to leave with him after work on Friday."

Lexy hadn't stopped pacing since she received the message. Rutledge approached her and gently wrapped his arms around her. "Breathe for a minute," he whispered. He never let go; he just held her. She started to take deep breaths, and he could feel the tension in her muscles releasing. "Let's sit back down." Gently grabbing her hand, Rutledge led her back to the couch.

"I'm sorry," Lexy started to cry. "I'm ruining another evening together with a conversation about George. I'm an idiot." She had been on edge all week, and the avalanche of emotions was finally being released. "I've been so scared all week. I hate being at home. I think George is going to show up at any time!" She was able to gain control of her crying, but even without the tears, Rutledge could see how upset she was. "I bet he knows about you. He's probably inviting me on a trip so that he can kill me. He's the one who deserves to be killed!"

Rutledge didn't want to chime in. He wanted Lexy to feel free to express her emotions. The mix of rage and fear she felt was understandable; he would feel the same way if he were in her shoes. He hated having been the one to tell her about George, and seeing how it was affecting her; he couldn't help but partially blame himself. "I'm going to make sure nothing happens to you," he promised her.

"I think I want to go with him," she stood and started to pace again. "He needs to be stopped. No one would know we were together on his boat, besides you. I could take a gun with me and end this all for good. I wouldn't have to spend another night afraid in my apartment. I wouldn't have to feel like he's watching my every move."

"That's not a good idea. If you get caught, your

future is over. You could be convicted of murder and end up with a jail sentence, or worse, he could kill you before you even have a chance to kill him. You would be putting everything on the line. For what?" Rutledge implored Lexy not to do it, but he could tell by the look on her face that she already had her mind made up. "You're not listening to me, are you?"

"Do you know how to shoot a gun?" Lexy asked. She clearly hadn't been listening. He was frustrated, but he nodded in response to her question. "Don't worry, I'm not asking you to kill George," she clarified. "I need you to teach me how to shoot. Before next weekend." With a pink notepad in hand, she started to scribble down notes.

Rutledge didn't know how to put a stop to her madness. "It's not worth it, Lexy."

"He's already responsible for two of his wives' deaths. I'm not letting him add more women to that list. He's a cheater, a coward, and a murderer." Lexy was afraid, but she wanted to take back control of her life. She didn't want to have to hide from George or be concerned that her own life was in jeopardy. She wanted her problem to be taken care of.

"If you are set on doing this, let me help you," Rutledge offered. Lexy cracked a smile, comforted by his proposition.

Chapter 17

"I think I have a plan," Rutledge announced, interrupting the silence that had filled the room. They had both been brainstorming, but it didn't take Rutledge very long to come up with a plan. He was more familiar with dramatic circumstances; it was his territory.

Lexy was intrigued. "Tell me," she said while turning to face him.

"If you decide to go with him, you would have to shoot him on the way down to Hilton Head. I could follow in my boat and pick you up right after it goes down. If something were to go wrong, I would be there to help you." Lexy had to admit, Rutledge's plan sounded flawless. It would be comforting for her to know he would be nearby.

"Could you help me figure out when or where I should do it? How detailed of a plan could we come up with?" Lexy asked.

"I could figure out the exact moment you would need to do it," Rutledge continued. "I could have you off his boat after it's done in less than five minutes," Rutledge guaranteed. Lexy's eyebrows rose. "What? I do this kind of stuff for a living."

"I know. You just seem very sure of yourself all of a sudden. Fear is healthy, you know." Lexy had enough fear for the two of them. Although she liked Rutledge's plan, she was second-guessing herself at the moment. As much as she wanted to, she wasn't confident that she would be able to go through with it. The anger inside of her was the only thing encouraging her. She kept reminding herself what George had done and what she felt he deserved. "Wouldn't it be obvious if your boat was following me and George? I think he would notice. He's usually pretty paranoid when we're together. He's always looking around."

Rutledge scratched his head, "I could always keep a safe distance and track your phone. That way I'll never lose you, but he won't catch a glimpse of me." Rutledge seemed like he had it all figured out. Lexy was partly kidding when she first brought up killing George, but now, it seemed like a plausible scenario.

"What would I do if George tries to kill me? How can I guarantee that I'll get the opportunity first?" Lexy had already made her mind up that George's invitation to Hilton Head was an invitation to her murder. Accepting his invitation would be putting her own life on the line. He could be planning the same fate for her as she was for him.

"We're not going to give him the chance," he explained. "Most likely, y'all will take the Intracoastal Waterway. Your best bet would be to try something when you reach the ACE Basin. The St. Helena Sound would be the perfect spot. The sound is long and wide, like an open ocean. It'll be dark by the time you make it there, and no one should be around." It almost sounded like Rutledge had done the very same thing before.

They were moving too quickly for Lexy, and she was starting to feel overwhelmed. "I don't even know how to hold a gun. I'll probably miss, and then he'll attack me. I'll be too afraid," she looked down at her lap as if it were shameful to admit it.

"Look, I don't want you to do this. I'd truly prefer you not. I wanted to prepare you, if you were going to, that's all. We don't need to talk about this for another minute. We'll figure out another solution," he put his arm around Lexy, and she rested her head on his shoulder. "You should probably let him know that you're not going to go with him. The longer you wait, the worse he will react I'm afraid."

Lexy pulled away from Rutledge, "I still haven't decided." Her eyes darted to the large windows in front of them. The curtains were still drawn, but she felt like someone was watching them. She was sick of being afraid. If she didn't do something, she would always be looking over her shoulder. "Do you think your plan is foolproof?"

"I do," Rutledge looked her dead in the eye. "I care more about you than you know. I wouldn't let anything bad happen to you."

Part of her was hoping Rutledge would volunteer to take care of George himself, but it was a lot to expect from someone she barely knew. Shooting George had been her idea, and Rutledge was only trying to help. It was not his battle; it was Lexy's. "Will you teach me how to shoot a gun tomorrow?" She hadn't decided whether or not she was going to go through with the plan, but she figured learning how to shoot a gun in preparation wouldn't hurt.

"I can do that. You're going to need a gun though." Rutledge had a few of his own, but he didn't want to use them.

"I have a handgun! My dad got it for me when I moved into my first apartment." Lexy ran to her bedroom and returned with a small pistol. She was swinging it around, completely unaware of the proper way to handle a firearm.

Rutledge used a pillow as a shield. "Whoa, there!" He chuckled, but he was dead serious. "Why don't you just set it on the coffee table?" Lexy placed the gun down, and Rutledge exhaled sharply. "Did your dad not teach you how to properly handle it at least? There's no point for you to have it if you don't know how to use it."

"He gave it to for me like five years ago," Lexy pursed her lips. "He took me to a shooting range, but I don't remember much of what he taught me. I was hungover that day, and it was scorching hot. I wasn't interested in learning how to shoot it. Honestly, I assumed I would never need it." She almost started to cry again, but she forced herself to hold back the tears. "Oh, and I don't think it's loaded." Rutledge checked the loaded chamber indicator, and Lexy was right, it wasn't loaded. Nonetheless, he felt strongly that it was now his responsibility to teach her how to shoot. The weapon was useless for her otherwise.

Seeing how emotional Lexy was, Rutledge encouraged them to drop the conversation for the night. There was plenty of time to continue the conversation the following day, and George had been a topic of their evenings far too often. "You should probably sleep on it. We can figure things out tomorrow," he laced his fingers through hers and led her to her bedroom.

For most people, the conversation Rutledge and Lexy had that night would have killed the mood. The dark plotting and planning didn't affect them; their primitive and unrestrained lust knew no bounds. The rest of the evening was filled

with carnal pleasures, and they both fell asleep sa-
tiated.

Chapter 18

While they sipped their coffee on Lexy's couch the following morning, the plan they had been devising the evening before was the elephant in the room. Neither one of them wanted to bring it up, but both were silently contemplating the idea. Rutledge didn't want to actively influence or encourage Lexy's decision. If she decided on her own to go through with the plan, then he would be involved in every step along the way to ensure her safety.

"I need to head out soon," Rutledge took the last swig of his coffee. "I have a meeting with a client this morning, but I can teach you how to shoot this afternoon. That is if you're interested in learning." He was dancing around the topic still, but Lexy was grateful that he wasn't directly bringing it up. She wasn't ready to make a decision yet.

"I think that would be smart. I mean, you were right last night. I shouldn't have a gun without any knowledge of how to use it," Lexy carried their mugs over to the sink and started to load her dishwasher. "Regardless of what we discussed last night, I think I should learn to shoot. If you don't mind teaching me, I would appreciate it." She nuzzled into his chest. "I really wish you didn't have to go."

"I know, it does feel like there's always something that I need to tend to. It can be a nuisance, but I prefer it over a traditional nine-to-five. It allows for a flexible lifestyle, and I enjoy my freedom." His muscular arms pulled Lexy closer, and she could hear his heart beating. "My meeting shouldn't take long this morning. I'll swing by to get you around one."

While Rutledge was out, Lexy showered and got ready for their afternoon adventure. One o'clock came quickly, and before she knew it, Rutledge was back in her company. "I talked with my buddy; he said it's cool if we use his land for shooting. No one lives out there; we'll have it all to ourselves. It's up in McClellanville, about an hour from here. Maybe a little more. Have you been before?"

Lexy had gone to McClellanville once for an event with a former fling. She didn't remember much about it besides the sizeable oak trees, acres of swamps and marshes, and the bothersome mosquitoes. "Once, but I didn't see much. It will be cool to check it out." She was unsure if she would fare well with the bugs, critters, and other things she could potentially encounter. Rutledge had already proven to be outdoorsy though, so she knew she had to suck it up.

"I already packed everything we need. I'm ready to head out when you are," Rutledge seemed excited, and Lexy tried to match his enthusiasm. Once Rutledge's car was loaded, they headed out.

As they drove over the Cooper River, Lexy noticed there wasn't a cloud in sight. "It's going to be a hot one," she complained. Rutledge nodded, but he didn't seem bothered by the heat. She wanted to inquire about whether or not they were going to have access to a house, restrooms, or air conditioning, but she didn't want to come off as needy.

They chatted on and off as they drove through Mount Pleasant towards McClellanville. Once they reached the small town of Awendaw, Lexy knew they were getting close to their destination. Only woods surrounded them, and the number of cars on the road had dwindled. Rutledge navigated to McClellanville as if he had been out there hundreds of times. He didn't need a map or directions. Before long, they were pulling up to a large metal gate. "We're here," Rutledge announced as he hopped out to open the gate. The lock had a keypad, and the gate crept open after he entered the correct combination. "There's a small cabin a little ways in. We'll park there."

Lexy let out a sigh of relief; she was hoping

the cabin would at least have a bathroom. They were in the middle of nowhere, which was already out of the ordinary for her. As she glanced out the window, she noticed the thick woods that encompassed the dirt road. She regretted not asking more questions before agreeing to join Rutledge. Though, he was doing her a favor. "Is there a bathroom in the cabin?" Lexy finally got the guts to ask Rutledge, and she was desperately hoping the answer to the question wouldn't be disappointing.

"There is! Were you worried you would have to go to the bathroom in the woods?" Rutledge laughed at her, but Lexy's face remained serious.

"Yeah, that's exactly what I was worried about," she admitted. She felt embarrassed, and she wished at that moment that she was more laid back. "I didn't know what I was getting myself into today. I'm sure we will have fun though!" She tried to act cheerful, but they both knew how uncomfortable she was.

"You don't have to pretend for me. I should have prepared you better for the trip. Of course, you are curious about where we are going. I mean, every woman wants to know if there's going to be a bathroom. I haven't dated anyone in a while, and I'm a little rusty at it. I'm sorry." Rutledge kept apologizing, and Lexy had to stop him with an abrupt kiss.

"Don't apologize. You're doing me a favor

today, and I am grateful," Lexy said as they locked eyes. They held their gaze for a few moments, and Lexy felt something she never had before. It was like being kicked in the gut and hugged at the same time. There was no doubt in her mind, she was falling hard for him.

Once they reached the small, rustic cabin, Rutledge opened Lexy's passenger door and helped her out of the tall vehicle. He gave her a quick tour of the cabin which included a bathroom break for both of them. "There's a field about a half-mile away. That's where we'll shoot. Do you need anything before we head down there? We have the entire afternoon, but I figured we would get the lesson over with first thing."

"Are we allowed to drink while we shoot?" Lexy was genuinely curious, though Rutledge thought she was joking. "I guess not," she said after having her question ignored.

"Oh, I thought you were kidding," he said. Rutledge was taking their shooting lesson seriously; he expected the same from Lexy. "There's plenty of time to throw back some drinks after we shoot. It's not a good idea to mix alcohol and firearms." Lexy pouted some, but it was because she was nervous. She thought the alcohol might calm her nerves; it was her go-to.

Once they reached the field, Lexy knew she was out of her element. She hated the wide-open space, and she hated the silence. To Lexy, being alone on the water and being alone in the woods were two vastly different things. She didn't enjoy what the backwoods had to offer. She was more of a boat, beach, or pool kind of girl. Rutledge was busy setting up their equipment, and Lexy fiddled with her boots.

"I feel like we are in the middle of nowhere," Lexy broke the silence with her obvious statement.

"That's because we are in the middle of nowhere," Rutledge snapped back. He had been short with Lexy ever since they had arrived, and Lexy could sense something was off. Nothing seemed off during the drive; his demeanor changed as soon as they got to his friend's land. Lexy tried not to push his buttons since he was obviously aggravated with her. She leaned up against his Tahoe and waited silently for his instruction.

Once Rutledge had everything prepared, a smile appeared back on his face. "Are you ready?" he asked. "I bet this will come naturally to you. You were a hell of a fisherman." Lexy found his sudden change in attitude to be strange, but she was grateful that whatever had been bugging him was no longer. He handed her the pistol. "Keep it down," he modeled with his hands what he meant, "and never raise it if I'm standing in front of you."

Lexy nodded, but she felt uncomfortable

with the gun in her hand. Rutledge had set up targets that were only ten feet away. "Are we shooting far enough?" Lexy asked. Her breathing quickened, and her fingers that were wrapped around the pistol began to tingle. Her mouth was drier than the Sahara Desert, and she wanted a drink.

"If you were on the boat with George, you would only be a few feet away from him. We're going to start at ten feet, and then we will move it closer to about six feet. You need to know what it feels like to get a closer shot." Lexy nodded; Rutledge knew what he was talking about. It was about time she trusted him. The sooner she followed his instruction, the sooner Lexy would be relaxing, indoors, with a cold beverage.

"Okay, will you show me how to stand?" Rutledge wasted no time pawing at Lexy's hips, arms, and abdomen, positioning her into a sturdy stance. She giggled every time his hands met a new body part. "We're all alone out here," Lexy said in a hushed, raspy voice.

Rutledge pulled away from her, ignoring her advances. "Does that position feel comfortable?"

"Yup," she said flippantly. Lexy was annoyed that he was blowing her off.

"Make sure to squeeze the trigger," he instructed while showing her what he meant. "Don't pull it. Squeeze it. It'll result in a more accurate shot. Got it?" She nodded.

For the rest of the lesson, Rutledge tried his best to show Lexy patience. Her shooting skills weren't all that bad, but she was a challenge to teach. Once two hours had passed, Rutledge was confident that Lexy would be able to use her firearm given the need.

Chapter 19

Once they made it back to the cabin, Lexy let out a sigh of relief. They had no plans to stay there that evening, and Lexy was ready to leave. "When are we heading back?" she asked Rutledge. She didn't want to seem pushy, but it was obvious she was desperate to depart.

"Do you want to relax and have a beer first?" Rutledge offered. "We can sit out on the porch. We never got to enjoy the peace out here."

"No, thanks," Lexy had enough of their afternoon activity. From the moment they had arrived, she had been ready to leave. Since their sole purpose of coming was fulfilled, she saw no reason to linger any longer. "We can have one when we get back into town, at my place." She almost apologized but saw no reason to. They hadn't gone out there to hang out.

Rutledge seemed disappointed. After all, he had driven all that way. "I guess it'll be easier to get into town before the sun goes down." Without another word, they headed out.

Lexy fell asleep on their way back to Charleston, and Rutledge was kind enough to not wake her until they reached her apartment. "Lexy," he whispered in her ear. "Wake up."

Lexy's eyes slowly opened. "Did I fall asleep?" she asked in the middle of a yawn.

"I reckon you did," he smiled at her, and she felt calm in his presence once again. Whatever weird energy she had felt between them in McClellanville was long gone. She figured it was most likely her energy that had been off; she had been uncomfortable the entire time.

"Come inside?" Lexy batted her eyelashes at Rutledge as she hopped out of his car. He followed closely behind her without responding. Right when her front door shut, Lexy pulled her shirt off over her head. "I'm going to take a shower," she announced. "Care to join me?"

The two scrubbed each other clean, leaving no trace of their afternoon spent in the woods. They were once again playful and carefree. "Maybe we should check each other for ticks," Rutledge said as he let his hands wander all over Lexy.

After they playfully checked every nook and cranny on each other's bodies, they ate dinner and settled in for the night. "You don't mind if I stay here again tonight, do you?" Rutledge asked while they spooned on Lexy's couch.

"Not at all!" Lexy sat up quickly, allowing her eyes to meet his. "I would have you stay here every night if it were up to me, but I understand you're busy during the week." She gently kissed his lips, and for a moment, Lexy felt lightheaded. It was an odd sensation that came over her; she had never felt it before. "I love," Lexy paused for a moment, "spending time with you."

Rutledge's eyes widened; he thought Lexy was about to say that she loved him. To be fair, that is exactly what Lexy wanted to say. She had never said it to anyone before though, and she didn't know if Rutledge loved her back. She didn't want to face rejection. He pulled her back into their spooned embrace. "I love spending time with you too," he finally said. Although they both could have said more, neither of them did.

"Thanks for being patient with me today. I was a little out of my element if you couldn't tell." Lexy hated to admit that she was uncomfortable earlier that day, but she wanted to show Rutledge her authentic self. If he was going to fall for her, he had to fall for who she was -flaws and all.

"You're a better shot than I expected. If you did decide to go through with what we discussed, I think you would be just fine." Rutledge was the first to bring up their conversation from the previous evening.

Lexy had dodged the topic all day, but for

some reason, she was in the mood to talk about it. "I felt more comfortable with the gun in my hand than I expected to. The woods weren't my thing, but I did enjoy shooting. I thought about it a lot while we were out there today. I think I want to do it."

"You mean, you want to shoot George?" Right when the words escaped Rutledge's lips, Lexy threw a hand over his mouth.

"Don't say that. What if he has been spying on us? What if he can hear us?" Lexy frantically searched around her living room. "Where would he put something like that?"

"You're overanalyzing the situation. Trust me, he is underestimating you," Rutledge stood as well, but he walked right past Lexy to her refrigerator. After helping himself to a beer, he returned to his spot on the couch. "I've seen this before. He has no clue what you're up to, and I don't think he's suspicious of you. He might have seen me with you, but he probably assumes you found yourself a new hookup. I guarantee he has no idea what you are capable of."

"So we're a hookup?" Lexy ignored every other thing he said and zeroed in on the one thing that stood out to her the most. "I would say we are a little more than that."

Rutledge offered her a coy smile, "Of course,

we are more than that. I meant what George would assume."

The look on Lexy's face told him that she wasn't convinced, but she dropped it. They had more important things to discuss. "I think you're right though. He thinks I'm a bimbo. He wouldn't see it coming." Imitating Rutledge, Lexy retrieved a beer and sat down on the couch. "It's now or never. I need to make my decision."

"No matter what you decide to do, I'm here for you," Rutledge promised.

"I'm going to do it," Lexy said with sheer confidence.

"Oh yeah?" Rutledge looked doubtful.

"Yeah!" Lexy knew that there was no stopping her once her mind was made up. Rutledge would learn that soon enough. Neither of brought it up again and they enjoyed the rest of their evening. Rutledge had claimed the left side of Lexy's bed, and she was growing accustomed to having him sleep with her.

On Sunday, Rutledge didn't have any meetings lined up or any plans pulling him away from Lexy. He helped her with some light cleaning, they went for a walk, and they ordered pizza. Neither of them wanted Monday to come, but part of Lexy was secretly anxious for the week to start. The sooner Friday came, the better. There was no talk of George or the plan that Sunday, but they both knew that Lexy couldn't get it out of her mind.

When Monday morning came, Rutledge headed out when Lexy started to get ready for work. "I'll call you later," he promised her.

Lexy felt electrified. She hadn't told Rutledge, but she planned on texting George that morning to confirm the trip. She wanted to wait until she arrived at work to send the message, but she was too anxious. While applying her makeup, she sent the confirmation message to George. It said, "I would love to go with you! Miss you, can't wait to spend time together!" Saying those words to him made her feel sick, but she had to play the part. He sent a message back, "I can't wait! Call you Thursday to confirm plans." Lexy realized she had been holding her breath and finally exhaled, letting the air escape her lungs. She couldn't believe what she was going to do.

Chapter 20

From the moment her text message was sent to George, Lexy's stomach contracted into a tight ball and remained that way for the rest of her workday. On her way home that evening, Rutledge called her with some soothing news, "I'm free tonight. Can I make you dinner?"

Lexy didn't have an appetite all day and skipped lunch. A homemade meal would hit the spot. "That would be wonderful! Do you want to come over to my place or should I come to yours?"

"I'll come to you," Rutledge knew without having to be told that Lexy preferred spending time at her place. Her beauty products and clothes were readily available, and he didn't want to make her lug them back and forth to his place. She was higher maintenance than anyone he had ever dated.

"I'll be home in five minutes. Come over whenever!" The two hung up, and Lexy could feel the muscles in her body tense. She regretted not telling Rutledge before contacting George earlier that day. She needed to keep Rutledge in the loop; she owed him that to him if she wanted his help.

Lexy looked at herself in the rearview mirror of her car, and for a moment, she didn't recognize the woman peering back at her. She feared what she was truly capable of. The predicament Lexy was in was unlike anything she had ever dealt with before which meant it needed a solution that she had never tried. Lexy wasn't a murderer, but she also wasn't a victim. To her, she only had two options.

As hard as she tried to convince herself that George's murder was necessary, and for the benefit of others, she knew that what she was planning was horrific. Fear had driven her to the desperate plan, and fear would be the driving force behind her actions. She was sure that George would kill her if she didn't stop him first.

When Lexy pulled up to her apartment, Rutledge had just walked up. "Perfect timing," he said as he kissed her forehead.

Lexy had been in a trance the last few minutes of her drive, and she hadn't quite snapped out of it. "Hey," she said.

When Rutledge took a second look at her, he realized something was off. Her usually dolled-up face had minimal makeup. Her eyes were bloodshot, and her hair was in a messy bun. "How was your day?" He knew better than to comment on her appearance, but he was genuinely concerned for her well-being.

She waited until her front door closed behind her to answer, "I told George I would do it. I told George I would go. I've been freaking out all day." The words exploded out of Lexy. "I shouldn't have sent the text this morning. I should have told you before I did it; I set myself up for a horrible day." Rutledge wrapped his arms around Lexy, and she sank into him. "I'm not regretful. I'm overwhelmed," Lexy explained.

"I had a feeling you were going to contact him today. Well, we have a solid plan," Rutledge said with certainty. "We'll figure out the details over the next couple of days, and we'll have you prepared for Friday. For now, you're going to have to relax. Did you eat today?" Lexy shook her head in response. Without any further conversation, Rutledge made his way into Lexy's kitchen and began preparing dinner, "Good thing I brought some food over."

"Do you mind if I take a bath?" Lexy asked. "That is if you don't need any help."

"Go relax and enjoy yourself! I can't imagine being on my feet all day like you," he said. "I'll be here when you get out." Lexy walked across the room to deliver a single kiss on Rutledge's lips before disappearing into her bathroom.

Ten minutes into her bath, Lexy heard a light knock on the door. "Can I come in?" Rutledge asked from the other side.

"Of course," Lexy replied.

Rutledge handed her a glass of white wine immediately upon entering, "I thought this might make your bath even more relaxing."

Lexy took a sip, "You're so sweet. Thank you." She positioned the wine glass on the side of the tub. "Care to join me?"

"I would love to, but I have to finish making dinner," his eyes scanned her body, and she could sense his masculine urges. "I know what I'm having for dessert though."

Lexy shaved her legs and showered off before exiting the bathroom feeling brand new. Although the tone of the evening wouldn't be romantic, she put on a sexy number for Rutledge. When she joined him in the kitchen, his jaw dropped. "Like what you see?" Lexy asked him.

"I don't think I want to eat dinner anymore," he couldn't take his eyes off of her.

"Well, I'm hungry. I guess you're going to have to wait," she slyly smiled. Her cleavage was on display, and she tied the satin robe that hung off her shoulders a little tighter to cover up her décolletage.

Rutledge had already set the table, and Lexy liked that he was getting more familiar with her place. He seemed at ease in her kitchen. "I had some leftover crab in my refrigerator, so I put together some crab cakes. I roasted some potatoes and veggies in the oven as well. I hope that sounds okay to you; I probably should have asked what you were in the mood for."

"I'm not really a mood eater. Since I rarely prepare my food, I eat whatever is available and easy. You are spoiling me! I don't think I can stop for fast-food for dinner without a guilty conscience ever again." They both took a seat at the table, and Lexy wasted no time digging into her crab cake. "This is incredible. Can I hire you as my personal chef?"

"I don't think you can afford me!" he joked. "I'll cook for you any time you want me to."

"I don't want to ruin dinner by bringing this up, but I can't stop thinking about it. Are you sure you're going to be able to help me on Friday? I mean, are there even ways for you to track my phone?" Lexy asked.

"I already downloaded a tracking app; I can test it tomorrow when you're at work. As much as I wish I could take care of all of this for you, I have faith in you. George is making a mistake underestimating you." Rutledge was confident which in turn made Lexy feel confident. "I would never let anything happen to you, and you're going to have to trust me. With your life."

Lexy swallowed hard. There was nothing more to say. The plan was in place, and in four days, Lexy's problem would be gone for good. The truth was, she already did trust Rutledge with her life.

Chapter 21

Lexy's week went by at a turtle's pace. Rutledge had been busy every night since Monday, and she missed seeing him. The hours spent alone at night were unhealthy for her; she had come up with every way their plan could go wrong. She worried night and day, and by the time Thursday rolled around, she was ready to call the whole thing off.

On her way home from work on Thursday, her phone rang. It was George. "Hello?" Lexy said into the phone.

"Hey, sweetheart," George's voice gave Lexy goosebumps. It made her feel nauseous to hear him call her sweetheart. She wanted to say that he could go fuck himself, but she knew she needed to wait. She needed to do things the right way. Any doubts she had about the following day were gone. She was once again fired up.

"Hey! I'm so excited about our trip tomorrow!" It was almost painful for Lexy to fake her enthusiasm; she had a deep-seated hatred for George by that point.

George was buying her act, "I am too, babe! I was calling to finalize our plans. I don't think it's a good idea for you to meet me at the marina. The workers might get to talking, and rumors might make their way back to Penelope. I need you to meet me at a private boat landing. I will text you the address. Can you be there tomorrow right after work? Say, at six o'clock?"

George was making it too easy for Lexy. Not a soul would see them leave together. No one would suspect her. Lexy realized at that moment that she was hijacking George's plan; his plan to get Lexy alone and to kill her. She would outsmart him, and he would become the victim of his own game. "That sounds perfect. I'll take an Uber there so that I don't have to leave my car. I wouldn't want anyone to come across it and wonder why it's there all weekend."

"Good thinking," George seemed surprised by Lexy's quick wit. He, mistakenly, thought she was simply a mindless floozy. He had never explored Lexy's qualities besides her impressive physique and effortless skills in the bedroom. That was one of the many mistakes George had made.

"Is there anything special I need to bring? Any events we will be attending?" Lexy knew it was a pointless question to ask, but she needed to continue to play the part. The more convincing she was, the easier of a time she would have. If only Rutledge could hear her conversation with George; he would be proud of her.

"You'll need some lingerie," George said in a hushed tone, "but, besides that, you won't need anything else."

"What did you tell Penelope?" she asked.

"There is a medical conference in Hilton Head this weekend. I am one of the speakers, so she didn't even think twice when I told her I was taking the boat down. I invited her, but I knew she wouldn't want to come. It's not her scene," he explained.

"When will we come back to Charleston?" The question felt odd; it was obvious they would come back on Sunday. He hadn't mentioned her needing to take any time off from work. She hoped he didn't notice how different she was acting towards him. He didn't know her well enough to even sense that she was acting peculiar.

"We'll come back on Sunday. You won't need to take an Uber home; I will drop you off on the way to my shift." George sounded genuine, and Lexy once again considered that she might have the whole situation wrong. "That is if you don't love it so much in Hilton Head that you decide to stay!" There it was. There was what Lexy wanted to hear. The statement, the tone, and the attitude behind it. He didn't plan on letting Lexy return to Charleston.

"Sounds perfect," Lexy lied through her teeth. "I'll see you tomorrow!"

As soon as Lexy hung up the phone with George, she pulled in front of her apartment and called Rutledge. "George just called me," she told him.

"What did he say?" Rutledge asked.

"We solidified the plans," she explained. "I'm meeting him at some private boat landing at six o'clock tomorrow evening. I'm going to take an Uber there. From how he was talking, we are spot on with our assumptions." Lexy could hear Rutledge breathing heavily, "Are you okay?"

"Oh, yeah. Sorry. I went for a run. I had a shitty afternoon and needed to let some energy out," Rutledge clarified. He wasn't typically a runner, but he used physical exhaustion as a form of mental therapy from time to time.

"Okay. I'm sorry to hear you had a bad day." As concerned for Rutledge as Lexy tried to sound, she couldn't fake it. Her only concern was that he was mentally prepared for the following day. "Can you come over tonight?"

"Of course," Rutledge already seemed to be in better spirits. "I'll be there in thirty minutes."

Lexy took advantage of the thirty minutes she had alone and prepared for her trip. While she was starting a load of laundry, she heard a knock at her door. Peeking out the peephole, she expected to see Rutledge's handsome face, but no one was there. She slowly opened her door to discover a dozen roses sitting in a glass vase on her doormat.

"Whoa!" Rutledge declared as he walked up. He looked just as confused as she did.

"Did you get me these flowers?" Lexy asked him as she picked up the heavy vase.

"Can't say I did," Rutledge confessed. Lexy rushed into her apartment with the flowers in hand and pulled Rutledge in behind her. "Is there a note with them?" he asked.

Lexy shook her head. "There doesn't need to be. We both know who left these. Someone knocked on my door maybe a minute before you showed up! Do you think it was him or a flower delivery service?"

"What does it matter?" Rutledge asked. Lexy couldn't think of any reason why it would matter.

"I don't know. I hate having him drop by unexpectedly. It makes me feel violated," Lexy knew she was being dramatic, but she did truly hate the way George made her feel.

"After tomorrow, you won't have to worry

about him for another day. This is why we're doing this," he pointed at the flowers. "You deserve to feel safe."

"I needed these flowers tonight." Lexy placed the roses on her coffee table. "I needed to be reminded of why I'm doing this. Did you test the app while I was at work today? Could you see me?"

"I tested it on a burner phone I got to use for tomorrow. It worked really well. I could see your movements all day. It was kind of fun, actually," Rutledge lightly blushed. "I like knowing where you are, and that you are okay."

"Wait, do I need a burner phone?" Lexy questioned.

"No, you're fine. I only got it because my phone is associated with my work. I can't download a tracker on it," Rutledge explained.

The concerned look on Lexy's face remained. "We're really going to do this?"

"If it will make you rest easier, we are really going to do this," Rutledge promised.

Anxious for the following day, neither George nor Lexy had an appetite that evening. Rutledge helped Lexy pack a small overnight bag to take with her on George's boat. It needed to appear to George that she had the intention of making the trip with him, and she also needed a place to store her pistol. They buried the gun under handfuls of lingerie. Lexy made sure to pack the ring George had gifted her; she wanted to wear it when she shot him.

Once her bag was packed, Rutledge held Lexy in his arms for the rest of the evening. Neither of them slept for very long, or very well, but they never let go of each other.

"I don't want you to go," Lexy wrapped her legs around Rutledge's abdomen as they sat in bed the next morning.

"I know, but you need to get ready for work. I have one meeting this morning, and then I am free for the rest of the day. We can be in constant communication; I'll only be a text message away. Don't forget, I'll also be falling closely behind you," he reminded her. "Whatever you do, do not turn your phone off." Instead of their usual good-bye kiss, Rutledge hugged Lexy. He held on for a few extra seconds, and Lexy felt a sense of peace from the embrace. It was difficult for her to know that the next time she would see him, she would be a murderer.

Chapter 22

After work on Friday, Lexy reluctantly left her car in the parking lot of her office and contacted an Uber to take her to the address George had sent her. The Uber driver was too chatty for Lexy's racing mind, and she politely asked the driver to stop talking. Moments before the car reached the boat landing, Lexy placed the ring George gifted her back on her right hand like it had never been removed. The second his boat came into view, she knew there was no turning back.

George greeted Lexy with a kiss and thanked the driver for delivering her safely. The Uber driver had already been offended by Lexy's lack of friendliness and chose to ignore George's words of appreciation. Lexy had left a lasting impression on the driver. The car drove out of sight, and George and Lexy were standing alone at the boat landing.

"Well, follow me," was all George said to Lexy. She followed closely behind him as he walked down a short dock to his boat. Helping her on board, he was already getting too handsy.

"Thanks," Lexy casually pulled away from the firm grip he had on her, but she hoped he wouldn't notice. "This is an awesome boat!" She knew compliments were the way to appease George for the time being. His ego never grew tired of hearing praise.

George's cruiser boat was much larger than Lexy expected. George rarely used it, yet his boat was nicer than Lexy's parents' house. A month before, she would have been impressed by it. Lexy had changed more than she realized since receiving the mysterious letter, and she had Rutledge to thank for that. He had been there for her through it all. She was beaming with joy thinking about Rutledge when George spoke up. "Let me give you a tour," he offered Lexy. Though, the tour was more for his sake than for hers. She politely followed him around the boat and pretended to be impressed.

When they made their way to the master cabin, Lexy nonchalantly placed her overnight bag by the side of the bed he would assume she would sleep on – the one farthest from the door. Butterflies swarmed in her belly, but she knew George wouldn't peek in her bag. The gun would be safe until she was ready to use it.

The next stop on the tour was the galley. There was a full galley kitchen, though neither George nor Lexy knew how to cook. Lexy assumed that Penelope had whipped up some fancy meals in the boat's kitchen. It made her feel a tinge of jealousy, but she quickly dismissed the feeling. She had no reason to feel jealous of Penelope. If anything, she should pity her.

"That's enough of a tour for now. Let's get this show on the road," George said as he made his way to the captain's chair. It was a truly beautiful evening, and Lexy admired the view as they pulled away from the boat landing. They had about two hours until the sun went down, and Lexy was antsy for the darkness to come.

While George started navigating down the Intracoastal Waterway, Lexy saw an opportunity to prepare for the evening ahead. "I'm going to go freshen up," she announced. George looked pleased, assuming she meant she was freshening up for him.

Once Lexy was alone in the luxurious cabin, she sent Rutledge a text to let him know she safely made it aboard George's boat. His response was almost immediate. He had kept his word; he was in his boat only a few minutes behind Lexy and George. Lexy glanced out the cabin's porthole, but she didn't see any boats nearby. She was relieved that he was keeping a safe distance; there weren't any other boats around them. Rutledge would stick out like a sore thumb. He was close in case something went wrong, and that made Lexy feel as comfortable as she could given the situation.

Lexy touched up her makeup and hair before rejoining George on deck. As she approached him, she noticed how relaxed he looked. He was at peace while he smoothly navigated the Lowcountry's waters.

George had taken the liberty of filling two champagne glasses to their brims. Handing her one of the glasses, he clanked his against it, "Cheers to being together again! I've missed you." Lexy smiled politely and sipped her glass. She wanted to say something nice to him that would convince him that she had missed him. As hard as she tried, the lies wouldn't leave her lips. She couldn't force herself to say what she didn't truly feel; she wanted to tell him she hated him. She wanted to confront him for his lies and manipulation. Instead, she hoped her friendly smile would be convincing enough.

Chapter 23

As she slowly sipped her champagne, Lexy could see her hand shaking every time she brought the glass up to her lips. Her nerves were getting the best of her, but she knew she had to act naturally. George was used to seeing her drink, and he would be suspicious if she wasn't enjoying her glass of champagne. Though, Lexy knew how important it was to have a clear head that night. She couldn't afford to be sloppy.

"I see you're wearing your ring. It looks gorgeous on you," George complimented his purchase, and Lexy had to force herself to not roll her eyes. While on their trip, Lexy had been overjoyed when he bought her the ring. Now, it seemed like a dirty souvenir of their terrible affair.

"I've worn it every day since our trip," Lexy lied, but George was pleased with her statement. He genuinely believed that she had worn it every day, even if they hadn't been speaking. George arrogantly assumed the ring he purchased Lexy was the nicest thing she had ever owned. He concluded that she would try to show it off as much as she could.

"I knew you missed me," George said with a crooked smile. Lexy hated his arrogance, but it was more fuel for her fire.

"It was hard to miss you when you kept un-expectedly showing up to my place," she snapped back. She couldn't help herself. She wanted to call him out.

"That was one time. I tried to call you first, but your phone was off. I was checking on you," he grazed her leg with his fingers. "You know me, I worry." His hand wandered up her leg and disappeared under her dress.

"I feel a little seasick," Lexy moved away from George, and he got the message.

Removing his hand from underneath her dress, he pretended to be concerned. "Are you okay?" he asked.

"Yeah, I'm sure the champagne didn't help." It was the perfect excuse to fend off the unwanted touching and to get her out of having to drink anything else. "I need to pace myself if you want me to be any fun tonight!"

George moved the champagne glass away from her, making it clear what his intentions were for the evening. They continued to talk, and George told Lexy all about the conference they were headed to. The conversation dwindled and finding a new topic was like pulling teeth. Neither of them was truly interested in what the other was saying. They didn't have much in common, and their conversations had never been good, to begin with. Lexy had a nervous habit of chewing her lips, and after that dreadful evening, her lips were going to be raw.

The next hour went by painfully slow; Lexy was anxious to reach the ACE Basin, and George was overly chatty. George talked about work, his wife, and his house. He spoke to Lexy as if she were his neighbor rather than the mistress he had been screwing a month ago. Though, the way he touched her to emphasize certain words, she knew he still lusted for her. His ego had been bruised by Lexy's rejection of him over the past couple of weeks, and he was attempting to put her in her place. He wanted to remind her of what he had; he wanted her to feel envious of his life. Though the more he talked about his life, the more Lexy felt sympathetic towards Penelope.

The more George bragged and carried on, the more courageous Lexy became. She not only wanted to protect herself, but she wanted to help Penelope. For the first time in her life, she truly felt like she was doing the right thing.

The sun started to go down, and the colors in the sky resembled a painting. The colors intensified as the sun continued to set, and Lexy loved every moment of the show from her front-row seat on George's boat. She was distracted by the beauty of nature and lost track of time. The finale of the sunset came and went, and the blanket of the dark sky quickly fell on them. "Where are we?" Lexy asked. Based on the time Rutledge said it would take, she figured they were close to the ACE Basin.

"We just passed Edisto," George answered as if Lexy should have known. "We're near the St. Helena Sound." As soon as Lexy heard George mention the sound, a jolt of energy rushed through her body. She knew the time had come.

"I need to use the ladies' room. Be right back!" Lexy kissed George and let her lips linger on his for longer than usual. It was torture for Lexy, but she needed him to trust her. He smiled devilishly at her as she scurried to the cabin's bathroom. Not one ounce of him was suspicious of her. She had him right where she wanted him.

Lexy was lightheaded as she retrieved her weapon. For a moment, she panicked. She hadn't rehearsed how she would do it or what she would say. She didn't know if she should walk out and shoot him point-blank or if she should deliver a speech before the bullet. Everything else had been so carefully planned, she couldn't believe she hadn't practiced, or even considered, the actual act.

Whether or not she was ready, she knew it had to happen sooner than later. Nothing could truly prepare her for what she was about to do. Lexy sent Rutledge the message they both had been waiting for; the time had come for her to take care of George.

After taking off her clanky shoes, she gripped the pistol behind her back. Careful to not make any noise, she snuck back up to the deck. Her bare feet were silent against the cold floor, and the light wind disguised her deep breathing. Lexy didn't want George to see her coming; she wanted to catch him off guard. Her heart stopped when she noticed the place they had been sitting together only moments ago was empty. She hadn't planned on him moving.

Scanning her surroundings, her eyes darted to the bow of the boat. She noticed a dark figure leaning against the railing; George looked peaceful and gentle under the starlit sky. The distance George stood from her was about the same that she stood while practicing shooting targets only days prior. Only this time, her target was a living, breathing man. He was staring out towards the sky, and she wondered what he was thinking about.

For a moment, Lexy saw a man she used to love. She saw a man who made her feel special and sexy. She saw a brilliant doctor and colleague.

All the positive thoughts were pushed out of her head when she thought about the letter she had received. George was a monster.

The man standing in front of her was a stranger. He was an enemy. She felt her finger slowly move towards the trigger. Partnered with a deep exhale, she fired the weapon.

Chapter 24

George was caught off guard when the bullet struck him. His body tossed overboard like a rag doll into the dark ocean. Lexy froze in place. Her mind willed her to move, but her body was unresponsive. It felt as if she had weights holding her feet down. She couldn't believe what she had done; it felt as if she was watching it play out in front of her rather than experiencing it.

She thought she would hear George shout for help. She waited to hear his cries, but there was only silence in the water surrounding her. Finally, she regained control over her body and bravely made her way over to the side of the boat. Gripping the railing, she peeked over. The tide was high, and the ocean was calmer than she expected. She searched for any sign of disturbed water, but she saw nothing.

Suddenly, a single hand thrust its way above the water's surface. It was as if George was trying to crawl his way out of the water. His hand disappeared once again beneath the surface never to return.

Rutledge's boat appeared seemingly out of no-where, and it was in the nick of time. He quickly tied his boat to the stern of George's and rushed to Lexy's side. "Are you okay? Get anything and everything you had with you. Now!" Lexy didn't even have time to respond to Rutledge's question before reacting to his demand. She was physic-ally unharmed, and that was the most important thing to Rutledge. He needed to get her off the boat and away from the crime scene. She did as she was told and retrieved her belongings, toss-ing them into Rutledge's boat. "Double-check that you have everything," he demanded.

"But, I-" Lexy started to speak but was inter-rupted by Rutledge before she had the chance to finish her sentence.

"Check again. Don't leave any sign that you were here. Did you drink out of a glass?" Rutledge made a valid point, and Lexy immediately felt like an idiot. She shamefully retrieved the cham-pagne glass she had sipped out of earlier and did a quick once-over of the boat.

With the champagne glass in tow, she re-turned to Rutledge. "I have everything. I'm sure of it. Let's go." Within five minutes of Rutledge ar-riving at George's boat, the two of them were off into the night without a trace. Instead of heading right back to Charleston, they did a lap around the area to check for any nearby boats that might have heard the earlier commotion. When they didn't see a single boat out on the water, they knew it was safe to head back home.

On their way back to Charleston, Lexy slipped the unique rose gold ring George had given her off her finger and into the water. Part of her wished that she had gotten closure from him. She wanted to confront George. She wanted to ask him questions, and more than anything, she wanted to hear what he had to say for himself. It was too risky to waste precious time talking; he could have easily taken control of the situation had she waited too long. She could have been the one overboard that night.

Rutledge never asked Lexy how she was feeling after shooting her ex-lover because the answer was clear. Lexy was mortified. Her hands hadn't stopped shaking since the moment she squeezed the trigger. There was nothing that could be said or done to calm her. Lexy needed time to process it, and Rutledge knew that all too well.

"I don't want to go back to my apartment tonight," Lexy said. "Can we sleep on your boat and head home in the morning?"

Rutledge slowed the boat's engine. "I know it's hard to sleep in your own bed after something like this. Hell, it's hard to sleep at all," he spoke from experience. "Whatever will make it easier on you, I'm okay with." He dropped the anchor and led

Lexy down to the boat's small cabin. Her body was still shaking, and he hoped that she would calm down in his arms.

"Thank you. I'm serious. Thank you, for everything." Lexy looked up at Rutledge. "I love you." The words came out clear and concise. For the first time, she didn't try to minimize what she was saying or make a joke. She loved him, and she wanted him to know.

"I love you," he said in response. Somehow, the two dozed off together. Between the uncomfortable sleeping position and the waves tossing the boat, Lexy barely slept.

Every time Lexy's eyelids shut, she would see George's limp body falling over the railing of his boat. Over and over again, she saw this haunting visual. It played on repeat in her mind. Around four in the morning, she got up and headed to the deck of Rutledge's boat for some fresh air. She sat there, alone with her thoughts, until the sun joined her. The sunrise welcomed the day with a splendid violet sky, and it was even more spectacular than the sunset the evening before. Lexy saw it as a sign. It was a new day, and she was allowed a fresh start. She no longer had a reason to be fearful.

Rutledge slept in later than Lexy expected him to, and she had too much time alone to think. Whenever she would glance down at the ocean water around her, she would see George. Part of her expected for him to swim up to their boat at any moment, but she knew that was unrealistic. George was dead, and she had no reason to be afraid any longer.

When Rutledge finally woke up, he wasted no time turning the boat's engine back on. "I'm sorry, I didn't mean to sleep for so long. I don't know how I was able to."

Lexy considered the fact that Rutledge hadn't done anything besides be her getaway ride. Of course, he could sleep. His conscience wasn't eating away at him like Lexy's was.

The relief Lexy felt when they pulled into the familiar Shem Creek was indescribable. After dropping Rutledge's boat off for storage, Rutledge drove Lexy home.

"Do you want some alone time?" He asked as they pulled up to her apartment. Neither of them had spoken a single word during the drive. There wasn't much to say at that point.

"I think that's best for now." She looked inconsolable. "Will you come over later?" As much as she wanted to be alone, she knew that feeling would last for only so long. She would want Rutledge by her side again soon enough. He agreed to check on her later that day before she vanished into her apartment. Once Lexy was safe behind her apartment door, she sobbed. It wasn't a silent, delicate cry. It was an earth-shattering cry, the kind done only once in a lifetime. With snot and mascara running down her face, Lexy dragged herself into her shower. Turning the water to the hottest setting, she washed the guilt off.

Chapter 25

As sick as Lexy felt over her actions, part of her was thrilled that her problem was over. She once again felt safe in her apartment. She could open her curtains, and she could walk out her door without the fear of someone waiting there for her. It was the sense of peace she had been longing for.

The silence of the room was bothering her, so Lexy flipped on her television. The last channel she had watched wasn't Bravo, surprisingly; the news came on instead. On her television screen was the last thing she expected to see: George's boat. George's body had already been discovered by a fisherman during low tide that morning. The local news was all over the story.

When Lexy picked up the phone to call Rutledge, she was surprised his phone was turned off. For the next couple of hours, she tried to contact him with no luck. Eventually, she decided it was time to head down to his place. Maybe his phone wasn't working or he had fallen asleep. Judging by the amount of sleep he had the night before, she didn't think a nap was likely.

Lexy threw on some clothes and walked a couple of blocks until she reached Rutledge's apartment. Shortly after knocking on the door, she was greeted by a lanky, elderly woman. Lexy was taken aback but still asked the stranger if Rutledge was available.

"Rutledge who?" The frail woman asked in return.

"Rutledge Campbell," Lexy replied to the elderly lady with confidence.

"There is no one by that name here," the woman said. Lexy looked over the woman's shoulder at the apartment. The décor was identical, and the furniture layout was the same. That was the place she had stayed with him, without a doubt in her mind. The only thing missing was Rutledge.

"My mistake. I apologize," Lexy backed away from the door, and the woman slammed it shut. Lexy could hear her locking it on the other side, and she didn't blame her. She would have done the same.

Lexy ran back to her apartment as fast as she could. As she ran, she wanted to scream. She didn't know what the hell was going on. Rutledge had disappeared from her life as quickly as he had come into it. When she attempted to call him again, an automated message played informing her that the phone number was no longer in service. Unsure whether or not he was in trouble, Lexy was frantic to get in touch with him. Though, she knew that she had no other information about him. He was nothing more than a stranger to her.

Remembering Shem Creek Marina, she tried to give them a call. She explained to them that she lost her friend's number and needed a way to get in touch with him, but they refused to offer her any personal information about one of their customers. She had assumed that would be their response, but she figured there was no harm in trying. Helpless and with no one to turn to, Lexy impatiently waited to hear from Rutledge. He had been her partner in crime; she was sure she would hear from him soon.

The weekend rushed by, and she returned to work on Monday as if nothing had happened. She still hadn't heard anything from Rutledge, and George's murder was the hot topic around town. Ever since the police deemed his death a murder, everyone and their mother was talking about it. Lexy figured Rutledge had bailed on her; she assumed he had decided she wasn't worth the risk.

Lexy's coworkers spent the day gossiping about George's murder. A few of them personally knew him, though none of them were aware of Lexy's relationship with him. As far as she knew,

Nora and Rutledge were the only people who were aware Lexy had been seeing George. Ever since the news of his death had appeared on her television screen, she had been looking over her shoulder. She was paranoid that someone would find out that she was the culprit.

Seconds away from having a mental breakdown, Lexy tried her best to keep it together at work. When she was finally able to leave for the day, she had numerous missed calls from Nora. Judging by the number of times she had tried to call, Lexy knew her best friend had heard the news about George.

The one voicemail Nora did manage to leave voiced her concern for Lexy. She was worried about how she was holding up; she had no clue that Lexy was the one responsible for George's death. Instead, Nora was concerned that Lexy was heartbroken over the death of her ex-lover. The sympathy in Nora's voice pushed Lexy over the edge, and she had to pull her convertible over. It took almost twenty minutes for her to regain her composure before she could continue her drive home.

Finally, she made it to her safe haven. Once she closed the door behind her, she swore she wouldn't leave her apartment again for days. She would call in sick to work if needed. She couldn't be out among the chaos she created. She refused to turn her television or radio on, and she steered clear of the internet for the remainder of the evening. She knew there wouldn't be any positive updates, and every single time she heard George's name come out of a news reporter's mouth, she felt sick to her stomach.

Lexy had come to terms with the fact that she would probably never hear from Rutledge again. She didn't blame him for escaping the hell she created; she wanted to escape it as well.

As horrible as she felt about what she had done, Lexy was confident that she wouldn't be seen as a suspect. She wouldn't be, or shouldn't be, on anyone's radar. Their dirty little secret would be buried with George.

There was nothing for Lexy to do that evening but sulk in her bath. While soaking and sulking, Lexy heard a knock at her front door. Every inch of her willed the person behind the door to be Rutledge. It had to be him. She wrapped a towel around her body and headed to open it. Secure in knowing it wouldn't be a surprise visit from George, she swung the door open before looking out the peephole.

Chapter 26

Two male police officers, accompanied by one female officer, were standing in front of Lexy when she opened her door. "Miss Price?" The female officer spoke.

"Yes?" Lexy regretted answering the door in her towel. She knew exactly why the police officers were standing at her door. The male officers looked her up and down, obviously impressed by what they saw.

The female officer pushed her way through the two men. "Miss Lexy Price, you are under arrest for the murder of George Thompson." She read Lexy her rights. "I will escort you inside to put on some clothes before we head down to the station. We don't want you trying anything funny while you're alone in your apartment."

Lexy nodded in agreement. She was shocked, but she knew it was best to cooperate. She re-entered her apartment, and the female officer followed closely behind her while the two men waited in the hall. No privacy was offered to her, and Lexy quickly threw on some clothes.

With wet hair and not an ounce of makeup on her skin, the officer placed cold handcuffs on Lexy's dainty wrists and ushered her out of her apartment. Lexy knew better than to speak; she would contact a lawyer as soon as she was given the opportunity.

Immediately after exiting her apartment, she was put in the back of a police car. She wanted to look around to see if any neighbors were witnesses to the humiliating moment, but she didn't want to know. She refused to look anywhere but down at her feet.

She was officially a suspect in George's murder. The drive to the station was silent and tense. She didn't want to seem overly emotional or not emotional enough. She didn't know the appropriate way to react to what was happening to her, and that made her feel even less at ease.

The officers were polite to her throughout the entire process and eventually delivered her to the detective in charge of George's case. Lexy was put in a small interrogation room that looked like it belonged in the 1970s. A petite man, who also looked like he belonged in the seventies, entered the room with a folder tucked under his arm.

"Miss Lexy, I am Detective Ian Mable. I am in charge of George's case," he announced his position as if he was the most important person in the world. "I am aware that you requested a lawyer, and we are currently waiting for your lawyer to arrive. In the meantime, I wanted to show you these photographs." He opened the folder and selected a few photographs before lining them up on the table in front of Lexy. "Does this scene look familiar to you?"

The photographs in front of Lexy were somewhat hard to make out. They had been taken at night, and Lexy had to pick up each one individually to take a closer look. In the second photograph she brought up to her eye, she saw herself. It was undeniable; it was a photo of her standing on George's boat with a gun pointed directly at him. The next photo showed the aftermath of the shot, and the third showed Lexy clearly looking overboard, searching for his body.

Lexy tried not to physically react to the photographs, but she was stunned by what she was holding in front of her. The only person who could have taken the photographs was Rutledge, but he would never. Would he? She considered his sudden disappearance. Suddenly, she started to piece it all together. "He tricked me!" She blurted out. "But why?"

"Who tricked you? Do you recognize these photographs?" Detective Mable wanted more information. He wanted to hear her say the words.

He could feel in his bones that she was guilty, and he was confident that it was an open-and-shut case.

"Rutledge Campbell," Lexy had no problem dropping his name. He had dropped her from his life just as easily. "He picked me up off of George's boat. He was my escape. We stayed on his boat that night, and then he took me home the next day. He helped me plan everything. I have text messages to prove he was involved."

"Miss Price, are you admitting you were on the boat with George Thompson on Friday evening?" The detective asked bluntly.

Lexy felt as if her world was spiraling out of control. "Yes, I was on the boat with him. I didn't do anything though. It was all Rutledge. I swear."

"Miss Price, these photos clearly show you holding the pistol, firing it, and the outcome of your decision to do so. Do you agree? Do these photos show that?" The detective was not buying what Lexy was selling. He was talking to her as if she was a child, and she hated that more than anything.

"Where did you get these photos?" Lexy questioned the detective even though it was his job to question her.

"They were sent to us anonymously," he answered.

"Let me show you the text messages," Lexy begged him.

Detective Mable considered her request for a few moments before agreeing. "Where is your phone?"

"One of your officers has it." Not a second after she spoke, a police officer entered the room and handed Lexy's phone to the detective. Lexy realized that others were listening to their conversation, and she stared at the two-way mirror, wondering how many people were standing behind it. He scrolled through her recent text messages before trying to dial a phone number. "The number isn't even in service."

"It belongs to Rutledge Campbell. Can't you look him up?" Lexy felt helpless. Her lawyer was taking forever to arrive, and she was having a hard time fending off the detective by herself. She was scared shitless.

For the first time, Lexy was completely at a loss for words. The detective could see the vulnerable state Lexy was in, and he decided to take advantage of it. "Look, if something happened between you and George, we need to know. If you were defending yourself, you have to tell us. We need to know what the situation was."

Chapter 27

Lexy couldn't keep her emotions bottled up for another minute. The floodgates opened as soon as her lips parted. "I received a threatening letter three weeks ago or so. It warned me about George and what he does to women. It said that I would be his next victim. A few days after receiving the letter, I happened to meet Rutledge at work. He told me he was a private investigator, and after talking some, I requested that he look into George and his background. Rutledge opened my eyes to who George really was. He was a monster! I promise I did everyone a favor. He had two of his previous wives killed. He got huge life insurance payouts from both of them. Look into it! You'll see."

"Miss Price, George Thompson has only been married once. There are no records of previous marriages, and he has never received a life insurance payout. We have already looked into all of this. There was no reason for you to shoot him. Was there? I'm all ears. Make me understand. I'm here to listen."

"I told you! The letter told me that he was going to kill me! I was going to be the next victim!" She started screaming at the top of her lungs.

"Why didn't you bring the evidence to us?" Detective Mable asked. "We could have handled the situation."

"Rutledge convinced me that no one would believe me. He was partially right," Lexy said sarcastically. It was true; Detective Mable was uninterested in hearing about the letter.

"Ma'am, we already have all the evidence we need. We have photographs of you shooting an innocent man. Is there anything more you want us to know?"

"You have to track down Rutledge Campbell or whatever his real name is. He has a boat slip at the Shem Creek Marina. I have a picture of him on my phone; you can go ask the employees there for his real name." Lexy was proud that she was able to offer a solution. "You have to talk to him before you assume I'm at fault." He allowed Lexy to search her phone for the photo, and she presented it to him.

"You're still under arrest, Miss Price. You will have to spend the evening here. You're more than welcome to call a friend or family, but your bond hearing isn't until the morning. In the meantime, I'll look into the identity of your mystery man," the detective promised. "I never want to see an innocent person go to jail. If this guy was involved, I want him brought to justice as well."

The evening spent in a crowded holding cell was a miserable experience for Lexy. When the time came for her bond hearing, she was ecstatic to leave the cell. Her enthusiasm quickly faded when she heard the judge set her bail. It was much higher than she expected, and she knew her parents wouldn't be able to afford it.

She was escorted to change into an orange jumpsuit and was placed in a different cell. It was much smaller than the holding cell, but at least she was alone. Stuck behind metal bars, Lexy had run out of tears to cry. Anger and resentment were eating away at her. She thought she had truly loved Rutledge. At that point, she didn't even know if what they had between them was real. She didn't sleep a wink that night. Her weeks spent with Rutledge replayed in her head. How could she have been such a fool to think he loved her?

No matter how hard she tried, she couldn't find a reason for his unforgivable betrayal. How could he disappear without a trace? Lexy could feel the color drain out of her face. She had been played, that she knew for certain, but she had to figure out why.

Lexy had an early meeting with her lawyer, and her lawyer regretfully explained that the evidence was too strong against her. Her best bet would be to take a plea deal. He even suggested they use an insanity defense.

"I'm not insane. I will not be using my sanity as an excuse for my behavior. I did what I did to protect myself! Detective Mable will track down Rutledge, and everything will be okay." Her lawyer tried to talk some sense into her, but she wasn't listening. She had already made her mind up.

The detective arranged a meeting with Lexy for later that afternoon, and she was thrilled to take a break from staring at the windowless walls inside her cell. She was hoping he had good news for her, but she was quickly disappointed. "We haven't had any luck locating Rutledge. The staff at the marina claimed that they have never seen him there before."

"They are lying!" Lexy raised her voice. "I was there with him the other day! Let me go talk to them. I want them to say to my face that they didn't see me with that man."

"They looked in their database for his name and didn't find anything. They offered their security footage. I guess I could look into it," the detective offered. "Miss, you know you can't go down there. You're currently in our custody. Also, this is a murder investigation; if you tamper with any evidence, you could be putting yourself in an even worse position."

"I've been there with him a couple of times in the past weeks. I can narrow down exactly what dates and times, if that helps," Lexy scribbled down a few numbers and handed the paper to the detective. "How did you know who I was? Did the mystery sender of the photos give you my name as well?"

"No. George's widow told us about his infidelities. She told us about you, his most recent affair," the detective explained to her. "That is how you become our main suspect."

"Fuck," was the only word that escaped Lexy's lips.

Chapter 28

A few months before George's death, Penelope Thompson had learned about his extramarital activities. It was a devastating afternoon, one Penelope replayed in her head often. She hadn't been suspicious of George; there wasn't anything that led up to her discovery of his affair. It was a sudden, painful realization that came as quite a shock.

Earlier that year, on a Tuesday in May, Penelope had driven downtown to George's office. She planned to surprise him for lunch; he had been working frequently, and she missed seeing him. She wanted to ensure that they had some proper time to sit down together to chat, even if it was a silly little lunch.

George was having much more than lunch during his break. Instead of a nice lunch together, Penelope spent an hour in a downtown parking garage, watching her husband with another woman. He was scrunched into the backseat of his car with a blonde bimbo, and Penelope couldn't take her eyes off of the car. Although she couldn't see anything, the motion of the car said more than enough. She waited until they exited the vehicle so that she could get a good look at the home-wrecker that was screwing her husband. She was unimpressed by the blonde who exited the vehicle, and she found that even more offensive.

She left the parking garage that day a changed woman. She had always viewed her marriage as extraordinary. The moment she found out her husband was a cheater was the moment she decided her relationship was anything but extraordinary.

Most of Penelope's friends had dealt with infidelity in their marriages, but she didn't think it would ever happen to her. George loved her fiercely, or so she thought. She felt ignorant for assuming that he was any different from her friends' husbands. She couldn't even admit to her friends that George was having an affair. It was the most shame she had ever felt in her life, and it was a secret she kept to herself.

Initially, when she saw George with another woman, Penelope wanted to run over to his car, smash the window, and claw the woman's eyes out. But what good would that do? That was the day she devised her plan.

Penelope wanted revenge, and she felt both Lexy and George needed to pay for their actions. It would take time, and it would be difficult to look at George every night, knowing his infidelities, but she knew she could do it. It would be worth it in the end.

For weeks, Penelope acted clueless when George had late night meetings and last-minute shifts at the hospital. The truth was, she knew exactly what he was doing. She knew that he had taken Lexy with him to California, and she even knew about the gaudy ring he purchased for her. That one stung a bit, but it gave her the extra boost she needed to finalize her plan once and for all.

Any time George was away from the house, Penelope would research Lexy. She found everything she could know about her. It was easier than she thought it would be; Lexy was an open book. Her social media accounts told Penelope everything she needed to know about her and more.

Penelope had to pretend to be the doting wife she had always been. George never expected a thing. If he had known his wife better or had been paying attention to her rather than women half her age, he probably would have noticed the difference. He could have stopped the catastrophe that unfolded.

While Lexy was in California with George, Penelope sent the devastating letter filled with lies to Lexy's apartment. She knew that a woman like Lexy would take the information and run with it.

The next step in Penelope's plan was to provide evidence for the contents of the letter. During her research, she found out where Lexy worked. She hired an attractive man named Taylor from Camden, South Carolina to pose as a private investigator. Taylor, known as Rutledge to Lexy, made an appointment at the doctor's office where Lexy worked and pretended to be a new patient. He planted the private investigator seed, and Lexy easily fell for it. She called him less than twenty-four hours after meeting him.

Luckily, a family friend of Penelope owned an apartment down the street from Lexy's. It was one of her friend's many properties, and she rarely used it. She knew her friend wouldn't be visiting Charleston anytime soon; she was currently in Europe. Penelope had a key and would occasionally go over to water her plants and bring in her mail. Her friend was unaware that Taylor used it as a fake residence for nearly a month; Penelope had it professionally cleaned after his stay. There wasn't a trace that he had ever been there.

As well thought out as Penelope's plan was, she hadn't planned on Lexy falling in love with Taylor. That was a bonus. Unfortunately, Taylor was hurt in the line of fire as well. He fell hard for Lexy, but he had to keep up his end of the deal. The payment he received from Penelope was more than enough to cover the emotional damages, but it still stung for him. He had taken part in sending the woman he loved to jail. She would never forgive him anyway, disappearing was his best option. Once Taylor had his check in hand, he retreated to his small town. No one suspected him; no one knew his name. Lexy was the only one being held responsible for the death of George Thompson.

Penelope's plan worked flawlessly. She tricked her husband's mistress into murdering him. Her husband got what was coming to him, and so did his mistress. Every time she thought about her wicked plan, she gave herself a silent round of applause. George's mistress murdered him. It was the sweetest revenge Penelope had ever tasted, and she couldn't help but be pleased with herself.

George was the only man Penelope had ever loved. Losing him was the hardest thing she had ever gone through. Though, she didn't consider the loss to be the evening he died. She lost George the moment she found him in the arms of another woman. Their marriage was forever tainted, and there was no going back. In Penelope's opinion, George deserved his fate far more so than Lexy.

Unfortunately, all of Penelope and George's friends learned about his mistress and cheating ways following his death. It was unavoidable since his mistress was his murderer. Penelope didn't want to purposefully tarnish his reputation, but it was inevitable. Charlestonians talk and word spread quickly. All of her girlfriends had gathered around her, bringing endless bottles of wine, casseroles, and consoling words. They treated her like a victim rather than the mastermind behind her husband's murder. She relished in their sympathy, soaking up every kind word she was offered.

After learning about his affair in May, Penelope took out a life insurance policy on George. She used his birthday as an excuse, but she knew what she was doing. Between a hefty insurance payout and everything George left her, she was set for the rest of her life. As much as she felt like she won, she also felt like she had lost. She had lost more that summer than she thought was imaginable.

Chapter 29

"That conniving bitch," Lexy said to Detective Mable.

"Who?" The detective waited for her to elaborate further.

Lexy didn't care to explain anything to him. She was still processing the information herself. Penelope had known about the affair the whole time. "George wasn't the one; Penelope was the enemy," Lexy said to no one at all. "She tricked me into killing him!" Lexy brought her knees to her chest, and her body started to rock back and forth as she sobbed. It was a game of revenge, and Penelope used Lexy as a pawn. Penelope won, and Lexy would spend the rest of her life paying for her actions. "She set me up!" Lexy started to ramble incoherently, and her lawyer once against pushed for a sanity defense, but Lexy wasn't having it. "I'm innocent!" Spit flew from her lips as she yelled at her lawyer. "You have to believe me!" She thought of the last moment of George's life. When she saw him looking up at the stars, her intuition told her she had it all wrong. She could feel his innocence. Sure, he was arrogant and cocky, but he wasn't the monster Lexy was led to believe he was. She should have listened to her gut. Instead, she would have to live with the regret every waking hour for the rest of her life.

"Look, the evidence says something completely different. Help us help you. What more can you tell us? How did she set you up?" The detective wanted to help, but the case seemed closed. He had his mind made up that Lexy was at fault, but a part of him was curious as to what kind of evidence she could supply.

"Did you find out Rutledge's true identity yet?" Lexy asked through her tears.

"No, ma'am. All we have is a half-naked picture you took of him in low light, no offense. I can barely make out the features of his face. It isn't much help to me, Lexy." The detective's honesty was refreshing though blunt. Lexy wiped the tears off her face and regained her composure.

She had to admit that he had a point; the picture she had of Rutledge was terrible quality. She cursed herself for not taking a proper one of him. She had countless opportunities but never did. As mad as she was at Rutledge for what he did to her, the idea of never seeing him again made her even angrier. She thought about the last time they were together. They had both said the three words Lexy had always avoided; it was a moment Lexy wouldn't be able to wipe from her memory no matter how hard she tried.

"Lexy's parents are here to see her," an officer announced upon entering the room. He interrupted Lexy's train of thought, and she was welcomed back to reality. Detective Mable motioned for Lexy's lawyer to leave the room with him, and he reluctantly obliged.

"We'll give you all some time alone," the detective said. Lexy's eyes pleaded with him to stay, but she needed to face the music.

Lexy's parents rushed into the room. Her mom put her hands on either side of Lexy's head, grasping at her hair, "Lexy, what is going on?" Seeing her mom inside an interrogation room agitated Lexy. She had done this to them; she had brought this chaos into their lives. Although Penelope was to blame, she would never be truly at fault. Lexy was the murderer; she was the bad one.

"I did it," she bluntly admitted. "I killed a married man I had been sleeping with. I thought I was doing it to protect myself. I had it all wrong. I'm so sorry. I can explain everything. Please, give me the chance." Lexy began to cry, but her parents didn't comfort her. They looked at her as if they didn't know her. After all that Lexy had been through, seeing her parents like that was beyond the hardest of all of it. They were more than disappointed; they were on the verge of disowning her. Both of her parents cried, though her mom's tears were uncontrollable. "Please, you have to believe me. Someone set me up." She begged them to listen.

Lexy's mom couldn't regain her composure, and her dad eventually ushered his wife out of the room. They never returned, only Detective Mable entered the room again. "She's distraught. You're her daughter though. There will come a time when it is easier for her. I promise."

Lexy could hear what the detective said, but she let each word go in one ear and out the other. She didn't care what he had to say. Lexy knew it was unlikely that her parents would return. She saw it in the looks on their faces; they would never forgive her. Her life was over, and she only had herself to blame. She had been so easily outsmarted, so easily manipulated.

Without a single person on her side, Lexy had lost all hope. Her parents refused to attend her trial, but to her surprise, her best friend Nora showed up. The disappointment in Nora's eyes hurt Lexy to the core, but she appreciated her friend being there for her. In the hardest of times, Nora still stuck by her side. Her loyalty was deeper than that of her parents, and it was something Lexy wouldn't soon forget.

The jury looked at Lexy as if she was the scum of the earth. After seeing the photographs of Lexy on the boat with George, they unanimously decided on a guilty verdict within minutes of deliberating. Lexy was sentenced to life in prison for the murder of George Thompson. She didn't shed a tear at the hearing, but Nora sobbed for her.

Leaving the courtroom that day, on her way to spend the rest of her life in a prison cell, Lexy passed by the classical beauty that was Penelope Thompson. She appeared perfect, from head to toe, as always. She was being interviewed by the local news with a smile on her face, and she dared to say how difficult it was to stay strong during her husband's murder trial. Penelope looked perfectly happy for someone who should be a grieving widow.

Lexy laughed out loud at Penelope's ridiculous statement. "You wanted him dead," she screamed at Penelope. News cameras began to swarm Lexy and Penelope as they waited for a response from George's widow. Penelope's lawyer accused the police officer who was in charge of transporting Lexy of not doing his job, and the officer ushered Lexy along in response.

Before she was out of sight, Lexy's eyes locked with Penelope's. They both knew what Penelope had orchestrated. Penelope taught Lexy what happens when the tides change in Charleston, South Carolina.

The End

Made in the USA
Middletown, DE
09 November 2020